RECUSAL

A Story of Love, Law, and Insider
Washington Politics

R.L. SOMMER

TURNER PUBLISHING COMPANY

Turner Publishing Company
Nashville, Tennessee

www.turnerpublishing.com

Recusal

Cover design: M.S. Corley
Book design: Tim Holtz

Library of Congress Cataloging-in-Publication Data

Names: Sommer, R. L., author.
Title: Recusal : a novel / R. L. Sommer.
Description: Nashville : Turner Publishing Company, 2020. | Summary: "Jake
  Lehman, fresh out of law school at NYU, finds himself swept into the
  political intrigue and moral dilemmas plaguing the nation's capital when
  he lands in Washington, DC, for a clerkship with the venerable Supreme
  Court Justice White"-- Provided by publisher.
Identifiers: LCCN 2019035610 (print) | LCCN 2019035611 (ebook) | ISBN
  9781684424962 (paperback) | ISBN 9781684424979 (hardcover) | ISBN
  9781684424986 (ebook)
Subjects: LCSH: Political fiction. | GSAFD: Legal stories.
Classification: LCC PS3619.O455 R43 2020 (print) | LCC PS3619.O455
  (ebook) | DDC 813/.6--dc23
LC record available at https://lccn.loc.gov/2019035610
LC ebook record available at https://lccn.loc.gov/2019035611

Printed in the United States of America

17 18 19 20 10 9 8 7 6 5 4 3 2 1

DEDICATION

For GLS with thanks for all her help.

28 U.S.C. § 455(a)-(b)(1) (2012)

Disqualification of justice, judge, or magistrate judge

(a) Any justice, judge, or magistrate judge of the United States shall disqualify himself in any proceeding in which his <u>impartiality</u> might reasonably be questioned.

(b)<u>He shall also disqualify himself</u> in the following circumstances:
(1)

<u>Where he has a personal bias or prejudice</u> *concerning a party, or personal knowledge of disputed evidentiary facts concerning the proceeding*

TABLE OF CONTENTS

TABLE OF CONTENTS

Author's Note

This novel and the issues in it are fictional. The action takes place a few years in the future. A sequel will follow the key characters twenty-five years later.

PROLOGUE

People ask us—faculty, friends, an editor we know at a major publishing company, even our kids—will we write a memoir together? Our personal story, and the story of our times, should be a book, they say.

It really will take two books to write our story—our falling in love at the Supreme Court, and that crazy year post-Trump in Washington, DC.

A whole other book could be written about our recent experiences twenty-five years later, again involving the Supreme Court, this time about the gender wars we were caught up in, in unpredictable ways during those times.

Between our work and family responsibilities, writing this first book took discipline and some healthy arguments, but we survived. "Let's see how this first one works, with the help of our son, the writer in our family," we decided. *Recusal* is our recollections looking back at our year in Washington working at the Supreme Court.

Sydney Emerson
Jacob Lehman

chapter 1

Transition Time

The walk from Union Station to the Supreme Court Building took only fifteen minutes, but Jacob Lehman felt as though he had come a generation or two considering his rearview memory of his simple family roots long ago in Austria, and recently in New Jersey at the turn of the last century. The meeting that brought him to Washington, DC, was with Associate Justice Richard White, his hero as a student and his prospective first boss, if only their imminent lunch interview led to the coveted clerkship he had dreamed of during the last year of his successful career at the New York University School of Law.

NYU was the school the Justice had matriculated from years ago and from which he always chose one of his clerks. Jacob— "Jake" to most people—was this year's candidate to be one of the two clerks the Justice might choose. He knew Jack Kroner, who'd graduated before him and was now the Justice's senior clerk, but only by name and face. Most of the Justices hired Ivy League law school graduates, but Justice White was loyal to his alma mater and always chose a top student from it, recruited with the recommendation of the dean, Earl Chambers, who had been his classmate. Jacob was near though not at the top of his class, but he had an outstanding record of very visible extracurricular activities and a modest but likable personal way that earned him the admiration of the dean, the faculty, and fellow students. In keeping with their longstanding practice, the dean recommended Jacob to the Justice early in his third year, and after being invited for his interview in Washington, Jacob made the three-and-a-half-hour train ride from New York City with a mix of anxiety, crossed fingers, and his best-looking dark slacks, blazer, and bright red tie.

Jacob had often walked past the Greek Revival Federal Hall at 26 Wall Street in New York City that had housed the first United States Supreme Court. Later, it had moved to a US Senate building in the nation's capital before it found its current home at One First Street NE, in 1935.

Jacob reached the grand white Beaux Arts edifice that now stood between the US Capitol and the nearby Library of Congress building and smiled to himself, thinking about the experience he was about to have. He arrived a few minutes early and stood on the sun-drenched wide oval plaza in front of the majestic white-marble court building. Flagpoles, fountains, and benches rested at either end of the wide plaza, from which Jacob viewed the facade of fluted Corinthian columns, supporting a spandral displaying the words Equal Justice Under Law. Above, in the architrave, were carved historic lawgivers Moses, Confucius, Salon, flanked by symbolic figures representing Means of Enforcing the Law and Tempering Justice with Mercy. On either side of the steps were two metaphoric figures, a female representing the Contemplation of Justice and a male representing the Guardian or Authority of Law. Jacob was inspired.

Guards at the security entry found his name on the list and pointed Jake to Justice White's chamber at the end of a quiet, cold, stone hallway on the second floor. Also on the second floor were the administrative and other Justices' offices, as well as a library reading room. A gym had been added years before on the top floor, used rarely except by Justice Richard "Whizzer"

White, and occasionally by the clerks, whose seventy-hour work weeks were consuming.

When he entered the Justice's severe sanctum, the secretary—a handsome, middle-aged woman, well-dressed, tall, and pleasant-looking, sitting behind a desk in the middle of the room—stood and greeted him.

"You will be Mr. Lehman," she said, offering a strong handshake and friendly smile. "I am Ms. Friedman—Nancy, the Justice's assistant. He is expecting you. Come and meet him."

When the pair walked into his chamber, the Justice, a burly and informal-appearing man, rose and walked toward Jacob, hand extended. "Greetings, Mr. Lehman, how was your trip?" Before Jacob could answer, the somewhat-distracted judge was putting on his jacket, taking Jacob by the arm, and leading him out of the office. "The Court sat this morning, and we meet again after lunch. Shall we go right off? I only have an hour."

Off they walked, conversing—about what, Jacob would never recall. He was too excited about meeting the great man. All he would remember was feeling that he was about to change worlds, from a common and parochial one to an elite and prestigious one.

Justice White's table was prepared for them when they arrived for lunch, and they were greeted by the elderly African American maître d'. They ordered from the simple menu—a club sandwich and coffee for Jacob, soup and iced tea for the Justice. Their conversation mostly centered on the NYU School of Law and the funded legal rights program each had participated in— Justice White as its first fellow, and Jacob as the current and the last. It seemed the clerkship job would be his, though the Justice had never said so in clear words to that effect. But the conversation about their alma mater and his habit of taking NYU clerks, along with his offering Jacob suggestions of where to live in DC ("close to Court, since that's where you'll really be living!"), certainly indicated so.

As they rose to return to the Justice's office, they passed a table where he noticed the quite-recognizable Chief Justice, Eliot Freeman, who was eating with a statuesque young woman. Justice White stopped and introduced Jacob as his next year's clerk. After that declaration, Jacob recalled little of their conversation. The tall, slim, white-haired Chief Justice stood and welcomed him warmly, adding, "And Jacob, please meet Sydney Emerson, my clerk and your colleague next year."

She stood, tall but less than Jacob's six feet, slim and wide-eyed. Jacob was awkward, clumsily so. She was dressed elegantly, more formally than Jacob. His eyes smiled, betraying a modest young man. "I've heard talk of Ms. Emerson," Jacob replied. "Apparently she's a legend in our crew of clerks, I read someplace. Top of her class at Stanford and Stanford Law, and a Rhodes scholar."

"Hello, Jacob," Sydney replied, offering a strong handshake. "Where are you from?"

"New Jersey. I mean NYU," he answered. "And mostly everyone calls me Jake."

As they left for Justice White's chamber, Jacob's mind raced, though his gee-whiz eagerness prompted the others to look down quietly as their groups separated. They all shook hands, and the Chief and his new clerk-to-be smiled as Jake and his new employer walked off together. Justice White returned to his chamber, and Jake walked back to Union Station.

On the train ride back to his past life in New York City, Jacob did find himself thinking about Sydney, though not as much as he thought about Justice White. Was he going to be snubbed or overshadowed by the Ivy League clerks and super-stars like that Emerson beauty? What a friendly, informal gent the Justice was. He realized, at last, that this clerkship was really going to happen.

chapter 2

A New World

Three weeks after Jake returned to New York City and his final semester at law school, the formal letter from Justice White, the one he'd been hoping for, arrived. The dean called him into his office and presented him with the good news. The clerkship would be his in September. Jake called his parents in Englewood, New Jersey, half an hour from Manhattan, and later that evening they came to New York City to celebrate the good news at Nicholson's, their go-to place for family celebrations. Jake had been away from his family home for seven years at college and law school, but this occasion seemed different to his mother and father, who would truly have an empty nest when their only son went to live in Washington, earn his own living, and thereafter become a guest, less a part of his family for the first time.

No one in Jake's family was a professional. There was no context to guide his new journey. They were the center of Jake's life, but they no longer would be, they realized.

"To our son, who we are so proud of," Jacob's dad toasted. His mother wiped away a tear and smiled.

"Thanks, Dad, Mom." Jacob smiled.

The Court's term officially began in early October, but work for the Justices had not stopped during its summer recess. New cases arrived regardless of calendars and schedules. Some of the past clerks had departed. New clerks reported for duty at different times. The remaining clerks who were staying a second year would indoctrinate the new crew throughout the summer. Many of them would take their bar exams—Jake did in New York City—before taking some time off prior to boarding the treadmill of the next chapter of their lives. Jake lived at home with his parents for most of that summer, his last with the full-time room-and-board attention his doting family were delighted to provide.

After the bar exam in May, Jake shared a week with friends at their family homes in the nearby Berkshires. They rode bikes on wooded roads, played tennis, swam, fished small creeks for the local bass, and at night drank wine around an outdoor, stone-circled fireplace. It would be a long time before Jake would do anything like this again, he knew, so he gave himself over to the fresh air and exercise, which led to long and restful sleeps.

After that week of relief and farewells to old friends, Jake set off for Washington to discover his own living quarters and for his indoctrination at the Court. The elder of Justice White's clerks had found him an apartment near the Court, a condo rental that had passed from clerk to clerk in recent years. His parents drove him to his new address and helped him set up the furnished apartment and added his few personal things—an old photo of Willie Mays; one of him and a group of smiling, disheveled, Princeton Lacrosse players holding their sticks; and his favorite old Scottish plaid blanket. Later, they hosted a farewell dinner for Jake at the Fairfax Hotel's sedate, wood-paneled Oak Room. They returned to New Jersey the following morning, and Jake settled into his first official "day in court." The place was quiet and underpopulated.

Jack Kroner—who himself had been in Jake's place the year before—was there to show him around the places he'd need to know: the expansive, quiet library on the third floor, and the dining room where he'd lunched with his Justice months ago and where he'd sometimes (when not at his desk) lunch with his fellow clerks. Ms. Friedman, the Justice's secretary in chief—there were others who came and moved on—had been the Justice's key employee since he'd come to the Court. She showed Jake the inner workings of the office and explained the general office work schedules. The Justice would be back from a mid-West Coast lecture series the following week. Jack gave Jake assignments to work into the office routine, and at last—he was there!

Most of the clerks met informally in their day-to-day routines, and this included Jake and Sydney, who ran into each other one afternoon in the library when he entered as she was leaving.

"Hey there, Jacob," she said, smiling as they passed each other. "I see you made it. Congratulations."

"And you, too," Jake replied. "Jake, to you." He assumed she hadn't remembered.

"Are you settled in?" Sydney asked. "I'm sharing an apartment on Seventh Street with Ann Horowitz, one of Justice Gorsuch's clerks. How about you?"

"I'm at the Pendleton, across the street from the Court. I'm living alone," Jake answered.

Small talk followed, and they parted with "see you around" greetings and big smiles. Jake was pleased she'd remembered him and wondered if, were they to meet out of the office, she might have a warmer, more human side, less aloof than she'd first projected. Might he have misjudged her, self-conscious of his inferiority in the big leagues of lawyering now?

They ran into one another again before the October term began, when there was a late-summer meeting of all the Justices, who had now returned to their chambers, and all the staff and clerks who were back from their vacations. They gathered in the large ceremonial room used by the Court when special occasions warranted. Jake saw Sydney at the long clerks' table sitting with her roommate, Ann. She acknowledged Jake with a slight wave and large smile.

When the Chief Justice concluded his welcoming words, the Justices introduced their clerks, noting their home states and past school affiliations. The Court's chief administrator explained some need-to-know information about payroll, vacation, and insurance for the assembled rookies and answered questions. Finally, all were excused. Jake walked toward Sydney, mulling over what he might say, but before he reached her she was amid a small clique of clerks. She saw Jake and nodded with a smile, but Jake waved back and moved on.

Late that afternoon, the clerks all met at the nearby bar, Scales, the hangout the clerks historically habituated when work allowed. It was a small, local pub that people on the Hill liked to relax in, and because it was so close to the Court, Court employees were usually there. Autographed photos of the Justices hung on the lobby wall.

Sydney was standing at the bar with a few of her colleagues when Jake approached them. "Can I cut in on this august group?"

They welcomed him. "Try the local IPA draft, Jake, it is quite good," Ed Masters, a fellow clerk suggested. And Jake did. When he picked up his drink, Sydney had moved to a booth with a few of their colleagues, and when they waved Jake over to join them, he did.

The conversation among the clerks was mostly shoptalk about their bar exams and their new lives. As Jake sat down, Sydney was being asked about her Rhodes thesis on judicial integrity.

"The basic idea is obvious, or ought to be," Sydney answered. "Lord Coke famously wrote in 1628 that "no man can be judge in his own case."

"Yo! Lord Coke?" one of their colleagues kidded. "Sounds like a rap singer."

Ha-has as Sydney continued. "Roman law, Jewish law, Justinian, Maimonides Code, our Supreme Court all now agree about preventing partiality and prejudice. So I'm thinking I could turn the thesis into a University Press Book."

"I just read a case on bail," Jake offered. "It held a judge could be recused if he orders bail, because the commercial surety bond for pretrial release creates a conflict of interests."

"How can that be?" Sydney, now serious, asked.

"Because a small percent of the bond fee goes to the court for its expense fund for staff, travel costs, though not to the judge himself," Jake explained.

"That sounds excessive," Sydney commented.

"I thought so, too," Jake replied, "but the Fifth Circuit just ruled in that case. Check it out in the petition for our Court's review of that opinion."

Sydney jotted down the name of the case Jake mentioned, Caliste v. Cantrell.

Jake hoped when the chitchat ended, he'd get the chance to offer to walk Sydney home to get to know more about her. He didn't see a ring on her finger, but she was probably engaged, or at least seriously dating someone. She sure was beautiful. The walk-home fantasy became moot when her roommate, Ann, joined them and they both said goodnight and left. Jake did the same shortly after.

chapter 3

Trouble in High Places

Not long after Jake's arrival at Justice White's chamber, when all the Justices and staff were back at work, an unexpected cloud appeared, hovering over everything. It brought with it consuming trouble that would affect the whole White coterie, and in a surprising way, Sydney.

When Justice White was a young legal star working for a prestigious New York City law firm involved peripherally in politics, he'd worked for President William Treynor, who at the time was a glamorous and popular senator from New York State. A senior partner, on behalf of the new celebrity senator, offered White the opportunity to be Treynor's first legislative assistant in Washington, grooming him—in their minds—as a well-connected partner.

During the three and a half hectic years White worked in Washington for Treynor, their relationship was close, as Treynor rose through the ranks of the Republican Party and touched all the right bases politically. Eventually, he was elected president, but by then, White had returned to New York City where, as planned, he too rose through the ranks in his law firm. Years later, he was appointed an appellate court judge in the Second Circuit, a prestigious position from which he was later appointed to the Supreme Court with the support of the president. White and Treynor remained friends in Washington, though as captives of their very unique official lives, the two rarely met socially and never politically.

Scandal followed President Treynor to the White House. An anonymous leak in a *New York Post* gossip column suggested that the glamorous President was to be charged in a forthcoming book—*Deserted* by Deborah Dawson, a wealthy New York City divorcée—with having had an affair with Dawson that broke up her marriage to a rich Republican hedge fund owner.

Washington had a long history of women claiming old connections to new presidents. A Republican political committee sought an injunction against the publisher to staunch the looming scandal, but that only magnified the media coverage. Dawson's publisher went to court to defend its right to publish. A public fight to censor any book invariably made that book a bestseller. Dawson's charge, now in court, went public as a result.

The President's political enemies seized on Ms. Dawson's leaked scandalous charges and called for a prosecutorial inquiry in New York for fraudulent personal misuse of his senatorial office in New York City (a state offense), as well as federal campaign finance law violations based on his alleged "dealings" with his glamorous "pol-friend," as gossip sheets called her. The charge was, she had helped her lover's campaign with her then-husband's unreported money.

Treynor decorously denied the affair charge through a succinct statement by his press secretary, who peremptorily told the aggressive reporters in the White House Press Room, "The President knew the woman, considered her to be a former professional friend, and this charge is baseless; it is a distraction to his work for the American people who elected him. It is headed nowhere."

When Justice White met the President at a French embassy event a week after the alleged affair went public, they managed a few private minutes when they could step off and discuss the

Dawson scandal. The President shook his head. "It never happened, Richard. God knows what was on her mind. Probably getting back at her roaming husband." There was little time for more private talk and less inclination on either of their parts to pursue it at such a public event.

"Talk later," the President said as he walked back to the partying crowd in the embassy's showroom.

"Goodnight, Mr. President," the Justice replied fondly. "Regards to the First Lady."

Partisan and cantankerous citizens' groups formed to attack and defend the jilted lady or the embarrassed President. Media pounced on the battle. "Nothing sells so well as a sex scandal in Washington," one sarcastic commentator wrote. "No one wants to read about the gross national product's latest figures or another tsunami in Malaysia over their breakfast coffee when a spicy lovers' quarrel is the alternative." Everyone had an opinion. A strong one. And the story wouldn't go away.

That flap continued to intrigue the public's attention when the President made an inappropriate joking remark as he boarded the noisy helicopter for a one-day trip to Syracuse, New York, to speak at the Maxwell School at the university. He yelled at reporters running alongside him, adding an unseemly, "Shall I pardon myself if the matter interferes with my important responsibilities in the White House?" He was referring to former President Donald Trump's irresponsible remarks, who had threatened to do just that when he was under siege in the White House. Then the plane door closed as the President left for his conference, hoping the story would go away while he was gone.

The story didn't go away, and the Conservative Society jumped in on questions related to presidential pardons, should one become necessary, pointing out that Justice White, the

President's friend and protégé, might be the fifth vote on the constitutional question about the bounds of a presidential pardon. Their claim referred to an earlier case when the Supreme Court suggested in a footnote that the Constitution's presidential pardon power was absolute. Justice White was not on the Court at that time. Some of his current colleagues were, and they were presumed to be evenly split, 4–4. The footnoted remark was considered in the learned academic community as "dicta," a passing reference in an opinion and not the central precedent of that case, and thus it was not binding.

The dramatic point the Conservative Society raised and the media followed was whether, as the ninth Justice in that imagined future case, White would be inclined to support his old friend and make law—5–4 law at that—on this esoteric but controversial pardon subject. The battle of the airwaves and public interest groups that jumped in on both sides of the issue continued. Would Justice White have to recuse himself from hearing that case because President Treynor had referred to former President Trump's earlier boasts that he could shoot someone on Fifth Avenue in New York City and not be held responsible, and pardon himself?

Justice White remembered disagreeing with the generally held view of the Department of Justice and the academic community that the President's pardon power was total. When the issue had arisen in the Nixon and Trump administrations, the legal consensus had been that there was nothing in the Constitution stating otherwise. White remembered thinking then that the reasoning was bizarre. "Article II of the Constitution didn't list everything a president could not do, only what he could. It should be obvious the Founding Fathers didn't want American presidents to have kingly powers," he'd remarked to his clerk.

Needless to say, the gross national product and the Malaysian tsunami news made it to page nine, if anywhere, in the ensuing major national press, and the majors were not far behind the yellow-sensational press in their coverage of the new sex story. In one of his first weeks after the Court started its work, Jake had just gotten his footing about office procedures when the news broke. The *Washington Post* published a recusal story by its prizewinning investigative reporter, Dennis McCarthy, based on the Conservative Society's leak, at the same time as the *Post* printed a cutting review of the about-to-be-published, salacious book by what the reviewer called the "mad matron." Dawson's charges against the President made the *Post*'s front page, while the book section in *Style* noted in passing the possibility that Justice White might be the one to decide the touchy censorship and possibly pardon questions, if the Justice didn't recuse himself in the intriguing Dawson censorship case that was headed to the Supreme Court.

The problem was Justice White was caught between self-interests and false images. The publisher's fight against censorship of the forthcoming Dawson book was consistent with White's principles about the unconstitutionality of prior restraint, should that case come before the Court. And White's personal view of the pardon power not being total was different from that of the Republican President. He would be damned either way. The projected speculation that he should recuse himself would suggest that he should hide his involvement with either or both of the issues. To complicate matters, his views on censorship and the pardon power were contrary to the President's, and he wanted no part of embarrassing him. "Damned either way," he complained. "To recuse myself leaves me subject to appearing to be biased and protecting the President, with whom I've rigorously remained at arm's distance. Not to recuse myself puts me on the wrong side of issues my friend the President and I disagree about passionately—free press and responsible use of the limited nature of the presidential pardon power. The Conservative Society claim publicly embarrasses me and/or the President, whatever position I take on recusal. They can't lose, and I can't win."

chapter 4

Staff Meeting

The bubbling up of this conundrum showed just how Washington, DC, and the federal government had become the "evil swamp," as critics had called it. At a board meeting of the Conservative Society, the search for a strategy to exploit the notorious Dawson matter was hatched, and it was a libelous scheme, if anything could legally libel a President, or Supreme Court Justice, who were deemed to be such unique public figures that only malicious untruths could even be legally considered actionable. The plan instead was to make public charges that would force Justice White—the President's protégé—to recuse himself and admit bias, leaving the Supreme Court to decide the censorship issue then under appeal. And wouldn't it embarrass the President if his former assistant refused to recuse and voted not to suppress the Dawson book? Justice White was a middle-of-the-road Justice—sometimes siding with colleagues on the Left and sometimes on the Right—often casting the deciding vote in the Court's 5–4 decisions. The Society lawyers correctly assumed that Justice White would vote against suppressing any book. Either way he voted would embarrass the President—failing to recuse and assuring the publication of Dawson's notorious book, or recusing himself, suggesting there was something to Dawson's charge.

The Conservative Society's diabolical plan was hatched and executed after the book came out. Pundits pronounced their conflicting positions about the Court's constitutional conflict, and the President fled to the Middle East with a planeload of media, followed by another plane filled with a high-ranking platoon of policy experts from the White House and State Department.

Would the Court—White included—rule in a decision in the Dawson injunctive matter, assuring release of the hurtful Dawson exposé, the media pondered? To make the matter worse, Justice White was expected not to side with the four Justices who had been part of the earlier case that seemed to support the blanket pardon power should that issue ever actually arise. Justice White was expected to vote with the liberals on the Court, outlawing prior restraint of the book, but against the president on the pardon power's limitations if it arose again. Because he was not doctrinaire, he was the Justice whom handicappers couldn't handicap with more than a guess.

This scheme was a classic example of why and how conservative operational organizations so often whipped liberals. Under President Obama, the outrageous pseudo-veto of his Supreme Court nomination of Merrick Garland by Republicans didn't even allow a vote on his nomination. But under President Trump one year later, the conservatives pushed Brett Kavanaugh through the process despite the serious claims against him and his alleged brutish conduct under examination by the minority Democratic senators. Now, it was the conservative Federalist Society that influenced Supreme Court nominations as the non-political American Bar Association used to.

The conservatives were smarter and tougher strategists. This time, they would ingeniously play bumper pool by bouncing the ball off both sides of the table to advance their true aim of politicizing the Supreme Court. The Conservative Society's tactic this time was to act as if they wanted Justice White to recuse himself and publicly air his "prejudicial" past as a colleague of the President. Then, the Society could make the claim, albeit false, that White was biased and prejudiced, even though his recusal would not help the conservative cause of fighting against the Dawson injunction and allowing the Dawson book to dominate the news. White would surely vote that way. And airing the moot possibility of White's predicted vote on limiting the presidential pardon power and politically weakening the President from protecting himself, as Trump before him had claimed the right to do, would associate two presidents who couldn't have been more different.

Either way, either issue, White's friend, the President, would be damaged. Finally, and this was their underlying goal, if White recused himself in this instance, as Justices could do on their own and not subject to review, he would then disqualify himself from other future cases, having now admitted he was biased and prejudiced where the President's interests were at stake. Further, he would be doing it peremptorily, not in the high-minded, more judicious way better thinkers preferred.

The letter from the Conservative Society arrived at Justice White's chambers, copying Chief Justice Freeman. It notified them that a formal motion would soon be made officially to the Court, and threatened, subtly, that if he failed to follow up on its recusal demand, its charge would be distributed at an imminent press conference. The letter called on White to recuse himself for "failing to meet the statutorily required impartiality and personally biased test based on your history and association with the President that would likely influence your judgment on these important policy issues should they come before the Court."

"What the hell is this?" his loud exclamation blasted from his chambers. "Ms. Friedman—get my clerks in here. Now, please! You, too, Ms. Friedman!"

The three concerned staffers tip toed into the Justice's chamber and sat down in a quiet cluster after closing the door as the Justice ordered.

"So, what do we do with this . . . BS," the Justice asked as he stalked around the room angrily while his audience of three read the letter. One by one, they read quietly and passed the letter around to the others.

"If I recuse myself, I give the Conservative Society credibility for their irresponsible position on my being biased in cases involving my former boss. If I don't and support the publisher's position on censorship, as I do, I hurt my friend and early mentor. And if the farfetched pardon question ever arises, I have to tell him he *cannot* pardon himself, despite the government's and the academic community's wrongful position that he can."

There was silence. Jake chose a bad time to make a joke. "It's like the infamous LBJ story," he offered.

"What was that?" the Justice asked.

"The story may or may not be true, but legend has it that during one of his first congressional campaigns, he decided to spread a rumor that his opponent screwed a pig . . . sorry, Ms. Friedman," Jake offered. "But then LBJ's campaign manager said, 'Lyndon, you know he didn't do that!' and Johnson supposedly replied, 'I know, I just want to make him deny it, which will be the news during our last two weeks of the campaign: 'CANDIDATE DID NOT COMMIT BESTIALITY.'"

The story was apt, but Justice White didn't think it was funny.

Silence returned to the clerks.

"I knew Ms. Dawson from the old days when she was working as a rich political groupie for then-Senator Treynor," Justice White admitted. "But they had no affair, ever! I can't believe the story." He continued, "When he was in Washington, she wasn't. When he was in the New York City office, he couldn't have private time, he was so overprogrammed."

The frustrated Justice asked his three aides, "So what am I supposed to do now? Tell the Chief Justice and the press I never had intercourse with a pig?"

Jack Kroner, as the Justice's senior law clerk, offered to be the statesman, so the judge could stay out of the awkward moment—if only for a while. He knew someone at the Washington office of the Conservative Society and would talk to him and attempt to put out the fire.

"I'll go to their headquarters," he offered, "and ask them what this is about, and what evidence they have to support Dawson's outrageous charge as their basis for their recusal claim."

The Justice responded, "Good idea." He added, "Jack, do it as soon as you can. I will not write my response 'til we know more."

The group broke up and returned to work. But the mood in chambers was solemn and distracted.

chapter 5

Visit to the Enemy Camp

The Conservative Society offices in DC were on the second floor of an old building facing Dupont Circle. Like most public interest organizations in Washington, their space was crowded with plain furniture and bustling with young men and women dressed neatly but informally—jeans, no ties, shirts out. Jack rode the elevator to the second floor and asked the young receptionist if he could talk to Eric Yancy, an assistant to the Conservative Society's chief executive, Michael Turner, who was based in New York City. Turner handled fundraising and national media, while Eric handled the Washington lobbying.

Eric was a brilliant and aggressive aide whom Turner often used as his alter ego. He and Jack had met once at a congressional hearing, where they'd discussed televised trials, a subject the Justice and the Society were both interested in and on the same side. When Jack and Eric were introduced, waiting for the senators to arrive and begin that hearing, they'd had a brief and collegial conversation, which demonstrated that Eric shared the viewpoint of Justice White, who had written about it earlier. Jack hoped Eric remembered him from that friendly introductory meeting and might have some interesting information about the New York branch of the Conservative Society's recusal letter to Justice White.

"Hello, Jack," Eric called out as he approached Jack, who was standing in the reception area. "Good to see you again." Eric was decades older than Jack, dressed in a more formal Italian suit—detached, standoffish, quietly reeking confidence.

"You, too," Jack responded as they shook hands and walked briskly toward Eric's cluttered office nearby. "Thanks for seeing me on short notice. I was in the bookstore downstairs and noticed the Conservative Society satellite office is here. Thought I'd say hello and call on you about an awkward question."

"I bet I know what it is. Sure, what can I tell you?"

"Well, the Justice was shocked to read your boss's letter and its charge."

"I'm not the author, surely you know, but of course everyone has discussed S.455 and the importance, we all agree, of making the meaning of the prohibition against bias and impartiality clear."

"Of course, we understand. Unfortunately, those words can mean anything, given that all the Justices have been appointed by some president and not asked to recuse themselves for that reason. And *all* Justices have personal views about all issues, many strong ones about controversial subjects," Jack added, pressing the point. "But where, if I may ask, did the specific charges in your letter come from, a trashy book? Have you even read it? Checked out its credibility? How interesting that now your organization is taking the liberal view on prior restraint, perhaps so the President can be embarrassed." He couldn't contain the sarcasm, now that he was saying it all aloud.

"I am not the person to reveal that, in a private conversation," Eric responded. "Surely you understand that."

"Yes, but you—or the Conservative Society—can't make such dramatic charges without any evidence, and no one in our office, the Justice included, has any information that would support Ms. Dawson's charge. On the contrary. None at all!"

"It will come out. But not from me to you, which would be indiscreet. I can imagine how you feel and understand your curiosity. But the details will be disclosed in the ordinary course, and in the proper manner."

"When is that?" Jack jumped in. "After his denial is established, but his judicial reputation as a friend of the liberal President is compromised?"

"I'm sorry, Jack. I can't say more." And with that remark, Eric stood, smiled, and reached out to shake Jack's hand, a friendly if final sign that their meeting was over.

Jack wasn't surprised, but he was disappointed this meeting had revealed nothing to shed light on the Justice's perplexing situation. Later, he had to bear home the bad news that his detective work, well-intended, had left the question of the day in the dark.

"Boss, my news isn't good. They are playing us."

"Ouch," Justice White mumbled as he gathered his papers to leave. "Thanks for trying."

The Justice's conversation later that day with the Chief Justice in his more formal and ornate suite was no more enlightening. Justice White told the Chief that he was "nonplussed by the charge, which was baseless." The Chief responded, "There is no assurance the case—either of those issues—will get to our Court." But the Chief added, "Richard, unfortunately this is the political game we all face. The protocol is for you to respond to the letter and copy me. The potential decision to recuse or not is up to you, as you know, and it is not reviewable."

"But that leaves me charged and self-defended with the public looking at me forevermore as—as irresponsible! Which couldn't be more wrong. What about the President's family? What do I say to them? To him?"

The Chief Justice shrugged. "I understand why you feel as you do—frustrated, insulted. I know the President's family is aware of the politics of his office and will be supportive. But I can't do more than stay out of the fight, and I will support you if I am asked about it."

chapter 6

The Connection Is Made

The select coterie of Supreme Court clerks was a secret society of future legal superstars—two for each Justice and four for the Chief, who had extra administrative duties. They worked like monks, seven days a week, usually from around 7:30 a.m. to late at night. They were in courtly cantons that even their friends and families rarely visited. This subculture shared a rarefied experience that would forever bond them as they inevitably rose in the ranks of their profession after this brief and intense experience.

The Gang of Twenty, as one of them sarcastically referred to this elite group of new clerks, was a diverse club. A couple more women than men, but close to half and half. A majority were from the East Coast, and most were from Ivy League schools, or very good ones if not—Chicago, Georgetown, and of course Stanford and NYU. There were a few married couples whom everyone liked in their rare times together. The married clerks' non-court life was particularly difficult, as their family complications were exacerbated by their work schedules. One couple hosted a Sunday barbecue for all, and another couple hosted a Halloween party.

Attendees were supposed to create funny costumes, but few did, and they were unimaginative—a few showed up in judges' gowns, Sydney and Ann came as witches, and Jake as the *Wizard of Oz* scarecrow.

On holidays, when the Court was relatively quiet, they might have an evening off to share with their single colleagues.

The singles grouped in couples and cliques, most often at Scales, and friendships developed.

When they did occasionally go to Scales, Sydney and Jake made a point of sitting with their colleagues in the back booths, where they all tended to congregate, or on quiet nights at the bar in small groups.

Sydney rarely went. She and her roommate worked prodigiously and usually went home to their apartment. They were both runners who needed sleep so they could do their early-morning runs in the dark around Capitol Hill, shower, eat breakfast, and get to the Court before 8 a.m. One evening early in their clerkships, Sydney and Jake encountered each other on the way out of the darkened building, and she agreed, at Jake's suggestion, to have a beer at Scales on their way home. "I don't drink beer, Jake," Sydney answered, "but I'll have a glass of wine with you, okay?"

Jake bought himself a draft IPA and brought his frosted glass and her glass of dry white wine to the booth where Sydney sat. They were both weary after their typical long day but found each other's company pleasant. Their conversation about parochial, personal events not related to work was a welcome diversion from their high-class drudgery. What wouldn't be more relaxing than reading petitions for certiorari asking for cases to be heard by the Supreme Court on appeals from federal circuit courts and state supreme courts? The Court heard one percent of the cases that came to it, about eighty cases each year from the about eight thousand petitions from lower state and federal courts, and most of the culling was done by the clerks.

One way or the other, Sydney and Jake got to know each other on a personal level. They found time some evenings to stop at Scales, where a group of them—all except the married ones, strapped for time as they were—could be found with drinks in hand, relaxing, gossiping, some flirting, until they went on their ways to their quiet, empty apartments to sleep and soon return to their arduous but stimulating routine at work.

Jake was disappointed to learn Sydney was going home to the West Coast for Thanksgiving to visit her family for an abbreviated but welcome break from work (her five-hour flights to and from Washington and Los Angeles would be occupied by the uninterrupted reading of briefs and legal memos between her and the Chief). They liked each other, that much was clear, and they talked long and engagingly about each other and their work at the Court. Jake had misjudged Sydney. She was just as beautiful and brilliant as he'd thought, but she wasn't a snob.

They made a date to meet for dinner the Sunday Sydney returned. "My time to buy," she promised.

Jake was flustered. "Only the beer," he replied as they departed. He walked her home and then meandered into the night, thinking only about her.

They did meet again, and again, after that first drink, and both would later come to realize they were more interested in each other than in their other collegial friends at work.

As time passed, Sydney and Jake were seen eventually as a clique of their own, liked by all but often very private. They couldn't have been more different. Jake saw her as a very human personification of the lofty reputation he had remarked about her when they met. She was a brilliant student, a standout even among the small group of overachievers she had joined in the clerks' clique. But she was never assertive or argumentative, and always curious, insightful, and modest, though strong in her commentaries at work about the important issues they were considering.

They worked together easily on opinions when their Justices were on the same side, or negotiating for compromises when they were on opposite sides. Sydney and Jake learned from their professional conversations at those times that they were on different sides of several issues. Neither was far from centrist, but when there were differences, Sydney was left of center, while Jake was more to the right. Sydney believed that Jake was smart and always well-prepared, a good debater. Jake learned why Sydney had such a solid reputation, and he enjoyed their intellectual banter. Debating those differences, to their surprise, brought them even closer together.

She grew to see him as open, kind, and low-key but surprisingly persuasive in discussions of serious subjects. Jake was different from other young men she knew—interested in her ideas, cute in a boyish way. She enjoyed his wry humor.

Jake and Sydney learned that fall that they had passed their bar exams in California and New York and decided to celebrate. Jake had heard first, and when Sydney said, "Let's celebrate," Jake said, "No, we'll do it when you pass yours."

When that happened, Sydney called to tell Jake, "I passed."

It was late afternoon, and Jake said, "Now we can have a toast!"

They made excuses at their offices and went to Scales, which was empty when they arrived at 4:30. Sal, the bartender they knew well, looked up when they entered, and called out, "Who let you two out before dark?"

"Quiet. Just open a bottle of champagne," Jake ordered.

"Who's going to drink a bottle of champagne in the middle of the afternoon?" Sal asked, as he reached into the refrigerator.

"You and us," Jake responded, and the three of them clinked glasses. The moment was private and eccentric, and that empty afternoon bar scene when all the world was away doing other things would remain in Jake and Sydney's memory book of special moments.

"Only 35 percent passed our exam," Sydney said.

"Yeah, yours was easy, in California," Jake teased. "New York passed 30 percent. Remember that next time you brag about your credentials." He smiled.

Sydney smiled back, and they clinked glasses again.

"My mom called me to say the list was published in our local newspaper of people who passed. 'Thought you'd be interested,' she said, full of love and pride as usual," Sydney reported. "What a way to conclude a part of your life."

"I have to confess, this isn't my first celebratory drink. You're not the first person I told."

"Well, you called your parents, right?"

"It's a whole story, Sydney. Are you ready for this one?"

"Tell me."

"I had just graduated law school, taken the exam in May. It was in late summer, before I got here—and someone told me that the New York bar exam results would be announced in the *New York Times* the following day. Knowing that only about 30 percent passed, and sure I would be in the 70 percent who didn't—it was the hardest exam I ever took—I couldn't wait for the next day.

"'What the hell,' I thought. I was in the city, why not try? So I walked to the *Times* building on West Forty-first Street, went to the main floor, and full of myself said to a woman at the desk, 'I understand the bar results are here. Please check this name.' I wrote mine on a piece of paper and handed it to her like I was someone who was authorized to see tomorrow's paper.

"'I'll be right back,' she said, and walked off.

"Now my heart was pounding. Casually, she strolled back in a few minutes later, and nodded to me, saying, 'The name is on the list.'

"I managed to mumble 'thanks' and left the building. My family didn't answer when I called them. I had to tell someone, do something, and didn't know what to do. So I walked round the corner to Forty-second Street, saw a bar, and walked in. No one was there. It was about 3:30, after lunch, cold and dark before dinner and end-of-work-drinks time. The bartender noticed me, and asked, 'Anything I can do for you?'

"'Yes,' I replied, 'pour two drinks.'

"'You and who else,' he asked.

"'You and me,' I replied. 'I just passed the New York bar exam.'

"Me and my newest friend hoisted one, drank our drink, and I walked away, ready for the rest of my life."

Sydney laughed at Jake's story. "What's the word for what you did? *Chutzpah?*"

"You got that right," Jake replied.

In their small world at the Court, Sydney and Jake were becoming an item, an inseparable couple. When they could get away from work, they were usually alone. One night, after they had gotten closer, Jake asked, "Hey, Sydney, I've meant to ask you how you got your name. What's your story?"

"No big story. My father's father was Sidney. He died the year before I was born. They were hoping for a boy, but wanted to be surprised. They changed the spelling when I arrived, and I became Sydney."

"Best surprise ever!" Jake replied.

"How did you get named Jacob—you have a family story?"

"Yeah, I was also named after my grandfather, from the old country."

"You had a shtetl grandpa named Jake?"

"No, it was Yankel. When he arrived here, he Americanized it to Jacob, and New Jersey shortened it to Jake," he smiled. So did Sydney. "Only in America."

They passed the Rubicon from friends to something more when he walked her home one weekend night later that fall after work. They were passing by Scales when she said, "My room-mate is out of town for the weekend. Why don't I cook us a late dinner?" Delighted, Jake stopped on their walk and bought a contribution to the evening, an expensive bottle of Montepul-ciano to accompany her homemade dinner.

Her apartment was clean and neat, Jake noted, in comparison to his messy and untended quarters. Sydney went to her room to change into jeans and a loose Stanford sweatshirt while Jake uncorked and decanted his bottle, found some wine glasses in the kitchen cabinet, and poured two glasses, set them on the table to breathe, and browsed her spare bookcase collection of law books, poetry books, and several framed pictures that looked like family.

"Looking at my small circle?" Sydney asked as she came back into the room. They both moved to the kitchen while Syd-ney took out of her refrigerator a casserole of chicken cacciatore she had made the weekend before, and slid it into her oven. She told Jake, "I cook several meals on Sundays so my busy workdays can end occasionally with a fine, if late, dinner." No junk food for Sydney, it was clear from her body, which bespoke healthy and hearty.

The heated food smelled divine. "You're a good cook," Jake flattered her. "Is there anything you don't do well?"

"I like cooking. My mom is a good cook. I rarely get the chance to 'dine,' but the cooking part is fun, even if Ann and I reheat and eat late."

They lit candles on Sydney's small table and slowly savored her dinner and Jake's wine. They talked about things and times and subjects outside their Court days. It started erudite and slowly became more personal, from a controversial criminal procedure case they were working on to their lives.

After their long and languid, chatty dinner, they cleared the table, and Sydney said, "Let's leave the dishes. I'll get them tomorrow." They returned to the main room and sat together on her long, cushy couch. They smiled.

Sydney reached out her hand to Jake, who took it and said, earnestly, "I've only known you a few months, and not much of that because we work most of the time. When I met you at the Justices' dining room, I was awed by you."

"Jake, come on. Awed? Really?" She squeezed his hand.

"Seriously, listen to me. I never said this before, and I most likely now won't say it well—"

Sydney interrupted, putting her finger across Jake's mouth. "Stop talking," she said seductively.

Jake couldn't stop talking. "Really, Sydney, I think about you all the time. I'm happy whenever we are together. I want to be with you all the time. I . . ." Again, Sydney interrupted. This time it was her lips across his, and their conversation stopped. At this moment, Sydney and Jake changed from being good friends to lovers.

Sydney was less shy than Jake and took the lead entering her bedroom, holding Jake's hand, and immodestly undressed. Jake followed, seeming to be the less experienced in intimate affairs. Sydney was calm, assured, obviously experienced. Jake was an earnest, ardent follower. Few words were exchanged, while their first passionate time together soon became their second. Each of them responded to the other with cries, and pleas, and directions, and deep pleasure.

The following morning, Jake awoke in Sydney's disheveled bed with no Sydney there. He didn't know where he was until he heard the door open. She arrived in her running clothes, holding a Starbucks bag of muffins and coffees. "Breakfast time, lazy. Time to rise and shine." She smiled over her shoulder as she moved into the kitchen to unwrap her offering, while her shower ran over an ecstatic Jake.

They talked all morning—about themselves, initially. They were now curious about each other's pasts, beyond their scholastic accomplishments. Sydney's mother had had her sister, Valerie, first, then a miscarriage before Sydney was born—a surprise, late-in-life baby. She and Valerie were far enough apart in ages that their lives never connected. As Sydney was the baby, her sister resented her getting so much attention. By the time Sydney went to school, her sister was in a different place. When Sydney was in high school, Val was in college, away from home. Sydney had become the family star. Val was jealous.

Sydney told Jake about her longtime boyfriend from the high school and college days, Ed Vector. They were "the couple." He was handsome and a highly recruited high school football tight end, she said. "Ed was a good student, not great—B, B+. And a handy fixer-upper at everything from his dad's truck to my mom's washing machine. We were inseparable in high school. Everyone thought we'd be a couple forever. He went on to college at Oregon State because it offered him an athletic scholarship, and eventually he went to their engineering school—a really good school. And meanwhile, you know, that's when I was at Stanford and Stanford Law. Seven years went by when we were always in touch but infrequently together. Corvallis, Oregon, is a long and boring nine-hour drive, more than three hundred miles from Palo Alto. We both had consuming schedules. His summers were occupied with football practice and a campus job for scholarship athletes. We dated other people, but managed to be together for homecoming dances and some of Ed's games. We drifted away from each other, slowly, reluctantly. When I won my Rhodes, we met for a sad farewell. He was switching late to engineering school, so there was no way he'd be coming to England for two years, and I couldn't resist accepting the Rhodes. We parted, teary, promising to write each other, remain best friends, and see what the future held for us. Here I am now, looking at a future I don't know."

Jake told Sydney about his life as a small-town kid, an only child, in New Jersey, always successful but not spectacularly, like her. "I had a partial scholarship to Princeton, and an offer—loan but not scholarship—to come to Yale Law School. But the Hays Fellowship at NYU won me over, and the stipend included a tiny apartment near the school in Greenwich Village. Social-life-wise, I was busy, but it just wasn't a priority. Lots of local girlfriends, but none serious enough to talk about now. So, your life isn't how you imagined it?" he asked.

"I don't know. I've been so programmed to work all my life, sometimes I'm not sure if I'm missing out on fulfilling relationships. I let my high school crush pass, and I never got serious with my Brit boyfriend when I was a Rhodes. He was on to a career there, and I knew I wanted to come back to the US. My family was a world apart from this kind of life, so I had no model to follow. I guess I figured I'd end up on the Stanford faculty and marry a divorced colleague with two kids so I didn't end up a spinster with no children."

"Jeez," Jake responded, "that doesn't sound so appealing."

"No, that's why I'm so happy I met you. My prospects were looking pretty bleak for a while there! What about you, Romeo? Who did you think you'd end up with?"

"I never gave the question much thought. I had other things on my mind. I guess I figured I'd practice law in New York City and end up with some high-energy Jewish girl from Brooklyn named Nola who was an art historian or worked for PBS and whose huggy, kissy family was like mine."

"Funny how things can happen," Sydney said, cuddling into Jake's arms.

"Yeah," Jake replied. "People make plans and God laughs."

They never left the couch, talking through the morning, and eventually fell asleep together again. They awoke cuddled in Sydney's warm bed in a cold afternoon chill, and returned, together this time, to her shower.

chapter 7

The First Compromise

Sydney called Jake on her private cell.

"Jakey, that you?" Sydney asked.

"That would be me," he spoke into the cell phone. "Only you ever call me Jakey, you and people from New Jersey," he told her. But she could call him anything and he'd light up with a smile.

"Can you get away for dinner tonight—at a reasonable time—on me?" she asked.

"What's up? You know me, I'm here reading until my eyes bleed. No deadline."

"I have good news and want to celebrate. With you!"

They made a date to meet at a restaurant in town they both liked, when they could afford the fare and time off. "Can you meet me at 7:30 at Drake's?" she suggested.

"Shall I pick you up?"

"No, I'm working late and coming straight from the office," she instructed. "You go home and put on a party tie. See you then."

"You're not going to tell me what your good news is?" he asked.

"Later," was all she said as she hung up, leaving Jake mystified but intrigued.

Geez, might she be pregnant?

Drake's was a Washington institution, particularly at lunchtime. Drake himself greeted regulars, assigning tables with the care of a White House social planner. A *Washington Post* group of editors and columnists were always seated at the first table people would pass, entering the one large, well-lit room. One big-name TV host had a special table reserved, and waiters knew his special orders. Visiting sports stars always got special attention, and Drake personally walked them to their seats, stopping to make introductions to the "right" people. Ordinary folks tried not to stare, but when a LeBron James or a Roger Federer or a New York City anchor was in town for a White House interview, or a George Clooney–type Hollywood actor working on a political movie came through, it was hard not to rubberneck. The gossip columns would note these occasions, giving Drake free publicity. Lunches were long and lush—part super-deli, part fresh fish and big steaks.

Sydney and Jake never ate lunch there, not having the luxury of time nor an expense account, but went for occasional dinners when they could to inhale the capital scene and look at celebrities and celebrity photos on the lobby wall. Dinners were more sedate—quiet couples, lobbyists entertaining lavishly, and occasional curious drop-ins like them, such as a tourist couple tired from touring and carrying travel advisory pamphlets, rubbernecking.

Both arrived exactly on time—she excited, he curious. When they were seated and had ordered drinks, Jake asked, "So what's your exciting news?"

Sydney was glowing. She shoved a letter across the table, and Jake read it.

As he did, the waiter set their drink orders before them, Jake's Hendrick's gin on ice and Sydney's chilled white Bordeaux.

Immediately, Jake looked up almost in shock. He knew he shouldn't spoil the moment for Sydney, but he was white, dizzy, dumbstruck.

Sydney asked, "So?"

Jake weakly responded, "How great for you. I'm so proud of you."

She asked, "So why do you look like your mother just died?"

Jake blurted out, undiplomatically, "Because my life just stopped." It was selfish, and he knew it the moment the words tumbled out. He looked down at his drink, despondent.

"Come on, Jake, make believe you're happy for me."

"Of course I am. I'm sorry for being a bad actor. I just can't imagine you being a professor at Stanford, and me—God knows where, doing I don't care what. I don't want to be, like, your old boyfriend left behind as your life develops. I'm sorry."

It was quiet. Then Sydney said, "That doesn't have to be the case. We never talked about it, and I don't want that conversation, wherever and whenever we might have it, at *this* particular moment. Come on, Jake, smile. I want to share a very special moment with you only. Doesn't that matter?"

Jake pulled himself together, took her hand, raised his glass, stared at Sydney, and toasted, "To my dear, dear friend, who will grace Stanford Law School, for sure."

Sydney smiled. They clinked glasses. Dinner arrived, and they talked about other neutral subjects. Eventually she returned, tentatively, to the issue before them—their future. "Does this letter have to mean we can't continue as we are? I may not be there forever. You don't know where you'll be. It might be California, if I'm lucky. There are airplanes." She took Jake's hand.

"From frequent lover to frequent flyer," he joked.

"Hopefully more, but let's take one event at a time. Tonight, it's my exciting offer." At this time and at their age, careers came before marriage, and families started later in many young lives.

The rest of that evening was quieter than Sydney had hoped for, hardly celebratory. They left together, quietly and more like old friends after a long day's work than lovers looking to the future expectantly. Jake's kiss goodnight when he left Sydney at her apartment was more resigned, more formal than romantic, and he walked away bereft.

chapter 8

The *Washington Post* Story

As if the night before wasn't troubling enough, considering Sydney was heading off to her future at Stanford when Jake entered the Justice's chambers at eight o'clock the next morning, Ms. Friedman was already at her desk, the Justice's door was open, and with a subtle shift of her eyes in that direction, she silently instructed Jake to enter His Honor's sanctum.

He wondered what was going on. The Justice usually didn't appear until 9:15, well after the clerk-serfs had quietly arrived, coffee mugs in their hands, ready for the long day's endless work.

Jake entered, and as he did, the Justice—jacketless, robeless, tie askew—looked up from the papers before him and asked, "What the hell did you have in mind, Jake?" sliding an open page of the *Washington Post* across his desk for Jake to read.

He hadn't seen today's paper, and his heart sank as he read Dennis McCarthy's story mentioning their conversation at a recent party, innocent at the time, but embarrassing at this moment. Dennis was a veteran Washington reporter. He was said to have three lunches some days so he could exploit his sources. From breakfast until late at night, Dennis was working until the paper's deadline.

In what was a casual, passing comment in a noisy room of partygoers, Dennis had asked Jake, as he arrived, what he knew about the question going around about the Justice's "ethical" problem. Jake knew that journalists in Washington were always working, but he was having a rare night away from the office where all the clerks seemed to live, and had come to pick up Sydney there. She'd told him she would be coming.

"That's a non-story story," Jake had replied. "I know nothing about that and doubt my Justice has any ethical issue," he added and walked off to find Sydney. But the article before him this morning alluded to a rumor about Justice White's ethical dilemma, one Jake had guessed he knew about but never said so to Dennis. The problem was that Dennis had accurately, but out of context, quoted him in his piece. "White's clerk said the charges were a 'non-story' story," reported Dennis, which suggested more than Jake's naïve words had meant. It wasn't a story at all!

"Judge White," Jake replied, "this was at most a thirty-second passing conversation at a large party, and all I said was there is nothing to his rumor. This is a bad-faith use of my answer to him. I know the rules here about never commenting to the press about our work."

"Well, a closed mouth gathers no feet, young man, and now we have a problem."

Jake stood there before the Justice's desk, humbly quiet, and the judge looked up from his paper and roughly nodded his head toward Jake. "Go. You must have work to do."

Chastened, and furious at Dennis, Jake left White's chamber and entered his cubby-office, placed his briefcase and coffee down on his cluttered desk, slumped into his chair, and sulked. *What do I do now?*

In the ensuing days, Ms. Friedman finessed calls from Dennis McCarthy.

chapter 9

The Conspiracy

With no satisfactory resolution in sight and time passing before the Conservative Society's second shoe dropped—this time in public—Justice White went back to basics. He called his former, now-retired law professor, Meyer Leibowitz, who was still at New York University in emeritus status. White invited him to come and stay with him for one night so he could "impose on your wisdom, my favorite law professor."

"Never an imposition, Richard. I'm not traveling much lately with my back problems, but for you, how can I say 'no' to a cry for help from my favorite star student?"

The professor took the New York City–DC train that Friday afternoon. Justice White picked him up at Union Station and took him, with Jake in the car, to his stately Cleveland Park home, encircled by a wraparound porch with a swing, and a small garden behind. Justice White had invited the Chief Justice to join them for a private working dinner, but he begged off. It was clear he needed to maintain his personal distance from his colleague's problem. The Chief knew Washington politics, and as savvy operators understood, staying away from a fight is the best alternative, if you can. And he could, claiming he had to do so "in the interest of judiciousness."

White's wife, Emma, knew Professor Leibowitz and greeted him warmly, took his small overnight bag, and offered him a shower, time to rest before dinner, or both.

"No, my dear, thank you," he replied. "I remember your fine cooking and won't delay enjoying it any time you are ready. And here," he added, taking a package from his traveling bag and handing it to Emma. "This is a classic, super dry sherry. You are not to share it with anyone."

Soon dinner was served on the candlelit, screened porch, just the four of them. It was informal, chatty, relaxed. To the sound of crickets outside, they reminisced about New York and NYU School of Law goings-on. When coffee and dessert were ready, Emma rose and cleared the table, saying, "I know Richard and you have things to discuss, so excuse me while I clean things before I get too tired to."

"Sounds ominous, Richard," the professor said, turning toward him. "Not a health problem, please God."

"No," Richard replied. "But I am anguished by a development, one out of my control—only Jake here and my staff know of it. I'm supposed to be a wise man, but I confess I don't know what to do about it. I need guidance, and there is no one I respect more than you."

"Oh my," Professor Leibowitz interrupted. "Now I'm on the spot. Tell me, and let's see what I can offer that will be helpful."

"It has to do with our Court's recusal law, a terribly vague one that no doubt is violated often, with no bad intent, and which I am now facing in a situation I have no control over. But I'm afraid people will be wondering about me in a way they never have. And have no good reason to."

"So, what's the problem, Richard?"

"The problem is that if I deny recusal for good-faith reasons, I am perceived as publicly ignoring the charges concerning my mentor, the President, who is accused of disgraceful behavior, and of covering up for him. In addition, if I recuse and don't sit on the case involving him, as his opponents argue, I'd be hiding the fact that I disagree with him about two important issues: censorship and the pardon power."

"What behavior? What hiding?" Professor Leibowitz asked.

"That I am somehow biased in a precedent-setting case that might come before our Court, one I actually would like to write about academically, the unconstitutionally vague, clumsy recusal laws—S.455—but can't now. You should read it and see what it means—it leaves it to the challenged Justice to say yes or no to any charge against him, and that's that. No appeal."

White continued, "The easy cases are easy, or not controversial. If I hold stock in Company A and its case is before the Court, I may or may not be biased or prejudiced—whatever those words mean—but for the appearance of justice, the question being a fair one, I'd publicly recuse myself without being asked. The hard cases are the tough ones. If Jake here went into practice and came before the Court on a case, as often happens with former law clerks, I would ask my colleagues—who have had the same question asked of them—if they agreed with me that I could adjudge the case without bias or prejudice. They'd agree I could."

"Then what is your problem that isn't clear or fair, and that troubles you?"

"Tell him, Jake," White instructed. "Show him S.455 and the Conservative Society letter. This is too painful to me."

Jake immediately handed both items to Professor Leibowitz, and he and his boss sat back. Justice White offered Leibowitz and Jake an after-dinner drink, and both declined. He rose and poured himself a small glass of his favorite bourbon, added a few pieces of ice, and slumped back into his chair.

After a while, when Professor Leibowitz finished reading the two pages Jake had provided, he laid them on the table, sat back, and after a long pause, asked, "What then is the problem? That the charge is right, or that it is wrong?"

"It is," White quickly replied, "that without any legitimate reason, we would be discussing whether or not my mentor was unfaithful, and that I am biased in the President's favor, and the American public will always wonder: Was he unfaithful? Is the judge covering up for his old friend? I'm damned whatever the answer is and embarrassed for no good reason. If I challenge the Conservative Society on the lower court's position on censorship if it comes up to our Court, when I think the injunction is wrong, or even on the President's use of his pardon power, which may or may not come up, when I think *he* is wrong, I'm screwed, twice."

White concluded, "If I do what is right and true and don't recuse, I screw my friend twice by honestly saying why I think censorship is wrong—exposing him to the Dawson book's bad news—and that I think he's wrong to say he could pardon himself, because he *is* wrong, but I don't want to chastise him publicly by saying so."

"I see," Professor Leibowitz replied. "Yes, how unfortunate for you. Let's explore options. What is the procedure going forward?"

"I went to the Chief Justice, who pointed me to the vague statute and stepped away. I should answer the Conservative Society letter, copy him as they did, and make my reply to them. If I have reason to, I recuse myself—asking the Conservative Society not to make their charge public. They had no good reason to demand my recusal, but politically will have won its claim. In addition, they know that without my vote, the Court is likely to rely on its past 4–4 pardon decision and leave the lower court ruling. I lose my honor and integrity pleading guilty when I know I'm not. Or, I fight the charge and win, because it has no basis in fact, but the result may hurt my good friend in the process by criticizing his protective views about censorship and pardons. 'Did you hear about the fallout between the President and Justice White?' will be the insider gossip in this small, tough town."

"Aye, yai," Professor Leibowitz muttered. "There has to be another way."

"We need to act fast. Bad news travels speedily in this town!"

"May I make a suggestion?" Jake asked the Justice.

"Of course. What is it?" White replied.

"You know the Chief Justice's clerk, Sydney? She and I are dating. And I know that she read with the remarkable Professor Horace Hartley in legal ethics when she was at Oxford on her Rhodes. She's written a brilliant—I read it—article that Stanford Law Review is going to publish. It has a section on ethics and judges."

"Wait. You didn't discuss our dilemma with her, the Chief Justice's clerk, I hope," White jumped in.

"No, I promise," Jake replied. "We are close. We discuss our Justices' work when we are working on the same case. She asked me to read and critique the galley of her article; that's how I know of it. I promise."

He continued, "She concludes S.455 is ridiculously vague about bias and prejudice, that it means whatever anyone reads into it. She offers better specific language Congress could use to avoid the issue when cases like Scalia's and O'Connor's and Thomas's arise."

"What are they?" Leibowitz asked. "I know that Thomas's wife worked on a case he heard and he claimed there was no basis for recusal. Scalia was challenged because of his personal friendship with Vice President Cheney when he—in his official capacity—was named in a case. He refused the request for recusal. What about O'Connor?"

"That was a classic," Justice White interrupted. "She wanted to resign because of her husband's bad health, but was waiting for the next election in case a Republican won and the new president could name a Republican like her to take her seat. Her husband admitted that fact. Then came Bush v. Gore, where she was the fifth vote making Bush the President—a consequential case, I'd say, and wrongly decided. When Bush was sworn in, she resigned, and he appointed Justice Kennedy to her seat."

"What would the Chief's clerk say in her book?" Leibowitz asked.

"The statutory language isn't clear, and the decision should not be up to the accused Justice to decide. The charge should be decided by a neutral ombudsman chosen by the Chief Justice or the Administrator of the Courts under his administrative powers."

"That makes sense," Professor Leibowitz responded.

"I agree," White added. "When is her bloody article appearing in the Stanford Law Review?"

"I can ask," Jake offered.

"Do," White instructed. "But no explaining why, except for academic curiosity, be sure."

"Yes, of course."

After Jake went home, Justice White and Professor Leibowitz sat up late, alone on the porch exploring as friends the Talmudic shades of debate about the quandary at hand, intriguing intellectually if one could keep one's personal distress out of the conversation. The night ended very late and without a final decision, but with an increased loving friendship between the Supreme Court Justice and his academic mentor, who promised to continue thinking about his friend's problem and consult if he had any useful ideas.

chapter 10

The Call

Less than a week later, when Ms. Friedman told Justice White that his "friend" from New York was on the phone, the judge put aside the papers he was working on and quickly picked up. "Is this my wise old friend?" he asked.

"Hello, Richard," Professor Leibowitz responded. "I hope you are well."

"I am, yes, though there have been better times for me."

"I had an idea, about our conversation a week ago. Not a legalistic or *aha* moment though."

"Tell me," the Justice replied.

"Well, if you don't think it is too obvious, I think there are ways to deal with improving the recusal law they want to use to make their case against you."

"Go on."

"Well, simple ideas can sometimes solve the complex issues, I thought," Leibowitz began. "Why not become the champion for reforming the recusal laws? Before their claim goes public, you make a preemptive strike. Get ahead of it. Call for Congress to change 455, define bias or prejudice more specifically, and *not* leave the decision to judges whether their conduct is ethical—or prejudicial. Better we have some system to leave that umpiring to a credible, detached decisionmaker—another judge, perhaps retired, and their decision is final and followed," Professor Leibowitz offered.

The Justice remained silent, thinking about what Professor Leibowitz had just said. "I see. I like it. Beat a scandal by getting ahead of it and adopting its point and offering the cure," White thought out loud.

"Sometimes we don't see the forest for the trees," Professor Leibowitz answered. "Put aside your personal quandary," he added. "I think the idea of having the Justices decide for themselves claims about their bias and prejudice is ridiculous—for judges, and most especially for Supreme Court Justices. How can this not be compromising?"

"What do you suggest as a way to do this?"

"Why not, instead of referring to your personal dilemma, or answering the Conservative Society's letter, take the high road by announcing publicly that in the interest of judicial integrity, future complainants, and the honor of the Court itself, reform of the current recusal law is important. Suggest it in a large, visible, academic forum, that all complaints against Justices go to a neutral arbiter, perhaps a retired Justice with an illustrious reputation, that he or she interview all sides, and publish a report, which the parties would have to abide by. Final word. No appeals. Recusal or no recusal."

"How do I do that?" White asked.

"Well, it could come up many ways. I could write to the Chief and Administrator of the Courts and suggest this, stating I was prompted to when I learned of your situation and looked into it. Or you could go to the Chief with your dilemma and ask him to raise it with the Court Administrator. The Chief has administrative powers and duties. Or, the dean here might suggest a law review panel on the subject, or invite you to address the Hays Fellows and faculty and students and New York City media. You can suggest your proposed reform—maybe there are better ones than yours. If NYU isn't interested—I bet we would be—you could try another academic venue, or the ABA, or a foundation like Ford. Lots of ways this could be brought up."

"You're wonderful, and I can't thank you enough. I knew you'd have a good idea. I owe you another dinner, and then some."

"You owe me nothing, my friend. If I thought you had no complaint, I wouldn't be advocating on your behalf. Holding your hand, maybe, but not advocating. You raised a question I hadn't thought of, was intrigued by, and being out to pasture, had time to reflect on."

"In that case, I want to graze in your pasture, as I always have. Many, many thanks."

Justice White hung up and called his clerks to gather to brainstorm Professor Leibowitz's idea. "We need to move fast, before the Conservative Society letter is made public. Let's try for the conference at NYU, which will like the idea and is the logical place. They have a big auditorium that has cameras to record it all, and the school could invite the hot-stuff, serious national press that covers the Court."

The staff hurried to their desks. At Justice White's suggestion, Jake began drafting the speech. Justice White called Professor Leibowitz, asking that he try out his idea on the dean. "Let's push this along, Meyer."

chapter 11

Oops

Jake loved the change of pace, working personally with the Justice on a matter of importance, away, if briefly, from the daily routine of the clerks.

One night after work, he and Sydney met in a booth in the back of Scales for a quick get-together over a drink, and he excitedly but confidentially told her what he was doing. When he mentioned he'd used some of her work on the Justice's speech, thinking she'd be delighted to be quoted by a Supreme Court Justice, she surprised Jake.

"Jacob!" Not Jake this time, so he knew he was about to hear her stern side. "I can't believe you didn't ask about this before you went ahead and used my work. You had my manuscript because I wanted—needed—some feedback and trusted you. You just went off and got brownie points from your Justice and didn't even ask me!" Jake had never seen Sydney so pissed.

He was taken aback. "Sydney, I'm truly sorry. I thought you'd be pleased to be quoted by a Supreme Court Justice and that your publisher would be happy, too! I never dreamed you'd be so possessive, especially in these special precincts."

"Just what did you appropriate?" Now Sydney was sounding like a lawyer, not his girlfriend.

"Sydney, I didn't *appropriate* anything, I just referred to a classic study of judicial ethics by an outstanding young scholar. I didn't use *any* of your words. I only referred to the recusal question—you don't own it." Now he was talking like a lawyer. "Of judges judging their own cases." He paused. Sydney quietly listened. Jake added, "I didn't plagiarize your manuscript, and I'm sad you think that."

Now the couple sat quietly in their back booth at Scales. Their mood had shifted.

After a long, quiet pause, Sydney responded, "I'm sorry. I should have known you wouldn't do that to me. I overreacted. I'm sorry."

"Our first fight," Jake answered perfunctorily. "Forget it."

"How can I make it up to you, Jakey?" She slowly, sexily reverted to her personal nickname, taking his hands in hers as she slid closer to him.

"Well, be creative," he smiled, loosening his tie. Later that evening, Sydney *was* creative. All was well again with the loving clerks.

Sydney was now a player, along with Meyer and Jake, in the rehabilitation of Justice White.

chapter 12

Caucus at the Court

Periodically, the Justices met privately in their oak-paneled conference room in the Chief Justice's chambers, with marble fireplaces and glass chandeliers sheltered by double doors. Book-cases of the Court's opinions lined the walls. They wore no robes and followed their routine that began with multiple formal but cordial handshakes. They sat around a rectangular table in black leather chairs bearing on its back each Justice's nameplate.

At the conclusion of one of the Justices' weekly confer-ences to discuss the assignments of opinions in pending cases, as everyone was preparing to leave, Justice White asked his colleagues about their approaches to charges against them for recusal. "Before we all leave, talk to me about how you deal with recusal questions." The Justices were gathering their papers, but White's inquiry struck a chord. They stopped their retreat, some still seated, some standing. One by one, the Justices aired their views.

The Chief knew what Justice White was referring to, but the other colleagues did not know about the Conservative Soci-ety letter, although they had seen the *Post* reports and probably guessed what White had in mind.

Normally, following the habit of their conferences, the speakers spoke in the order of their appointments to the Court, starting with the newest Justice and continuing finally to the Chief. They didn't follow that routine here.

Justice Gorsuch, the most recent member since Kavanaugh's departure, had surprisingly had to deal with few recusal clients. "I didn't come from private practice or the executive government," he volunteered, "so I haven't had conflicts from my prior work like Elena, who had been Solicitor General before coming on the Court. She automatically recused herself, though frankly I don't agree she needed to. Who doubted she could be judicious in her new role?" Gorsuch concluded, "I think that obvious conflicts aside, the presumption should be to deny, so we don't have 4–4 decisions about important constitutional questions. Who among us came to the Court with a clean slate, open mind, and no long-held views on the important issues of our times?"

"I could suggest a few Justices who know nothing about what they were called upon to decide," Justice Breyer kidded.

Justice Ginsberg called out, "No names please, Stephen." Others snickered at her remark. The popular celebrity Justice soon had to retire for health reasons after her illustrious career.

"But," Breyer added, "I don't want to have to give my reasons for recusal if I don't want to. It would only lead to more questions about my answers."

Ginsberg responded, "I've never recused myself, but if I was ever challenged, I would state my reasons publicly."

Justice Breyer, a veteran on the court, took the old-fashioned approach. "I have never agreed to recusal claims against me. They are a distraction—often political agitprop. Now, a claim by my wife's former husband . . ." he joked, generating an explosion of laughter from his colleagues.

"Seriously," Justice Alito offered, "I see little guidance in S.455 and am always uncomfortable sitting in judgment of myself. Like the proverbial shoemaker's children who have no shoes, we should be embarrassed every time recusal is called for, because, of all government officials, we are judging ourselves when prejudice or bias is charged, rightly or wrongly."

"That's why you are the unrecusal champion on our Court," Roberts kidded. The members were aware that Alito and his wife had a stock portfolio and that he had recused himself frequently when a company he had stock in was involved in a case. But most times, he unrecused himself after selling that stock.

"I go the other extreme," added Justice Sotomayor, former professor and lower court federal judge, "unless the claim is clear. I once held stock in a company whose anti-trust case came before the Court, and I followed the play-Caesar's-wife approach and recused. Those cases are few and far between, so why not avoid cynical clouds over what we do?"

Justice John Roberts, whose health problem had required he be replaced as Chief, had remained a Justice on the Court, albeit with a lighter workload. He backed the idea now shared by his replacement Chief Justice Freeman. "Our Court must always be above the fray, err on the side of neutrality. Justice White raises a good point, and we should consider altering S.455 as injudicious. I never felt I had to recuse myself every time my old law firm was involved in a case, any more than comparable questions arose about some former law professor or Solicitor General later on the Court," Roberts added, careful not to name names. "When I was Chief, I collected and analyzed recusal cases for one period so I could make my annual report. The typical reasons for recusal were previous work, ownership of stock, being named in a complaint, and family conflicts."

All eyes were directed to Justice Thomas, invariably the quiet member on matters of Court business. His wife was an activist lawyer in controversial matters that sometimes came before the Court. Thomas said nothing.

After a brief and awkward moment, Richard White changed the subject. "Well, I think the lower federal courts do a better job there than we do. When recusal comes up, their code of conduct requires transparency and review of their stated reasons, which bolsters the public perception of their fairness."

No conclusions were reached, no consensus evolved, and as the matter was not on the formal agenda, Justice White's solicitation for assistance with the problem he had in mind was not resolved to his satisfaction, or even edification.

The Justices drifted out, some alone, a few in small groups, and Chief Justice Freeman concluded to White, as they left, "Well, that wasn't a lot of help."

White replied, "No, it wasn't, but it makes it clear to me that we need to do *something* to clear up S.455."

chapter 13

Brainstorming with the Justice

Jake loved that Justice White chose to use him to develop his speech for NYU. It was an important one for him, and it could be influential. He was very interested in the three issues themselves—censorship, pardons, and recusal; the Justice knew more about the first two, but Jake knew about recusal from reading Sydney's manuscript. He spent parts of the next few days with the Justice, working in his chambers. One night they went to the Justice's home, while Emma was out of town, and shared leftovers for dinner. Their work lasted so late he ended up succumbing to the Justice's invitation that he stay overnight and drive back to the Court together the next morning. He loved the personal contact with the likable, if distracted, judge, feeling a personal bond growing between them. Jake never felt smarter than the people he most admired—Sydney and Justice White, for sure—but he had a competent and winning way they appreciated when they worked together.

"I'll get into the background of our recusal law," Justice White suggested. "I know anecdotal examples from conversations with my colleagues I can use from real life."

"What do you want me to do?" Jake asked.

"Remember the contentious Kavanaugh confirmation hearings years ago? The public was transfixed. You could use his remarks and the senators' cross-examinations to write a whole book about the inadequacy and absurdity of our recusal laws.

Didn't that brewery run an ad with his picture? 'I like beer, Senator. Do you like beer?' Ask your lovely friend if she has anything in her book about that that might be useful."

"She does," Jake replied. "I've looked already. This is going to be fun. I'll check with her how much I may and may not say," he added.

Jake was now chastened to the politics of his two important relationships.

He couldn't wait to get to the office the next morning. A good writer, he soon brought the Justice his draft of what he imaginatively wrote for his part of the assignment. He handed it to the Justice, who was at his desk, and sat down in front of him, waiting for the reaction.

"If we look back not so long ago, the confirmation hearings about Justice Brett Kavanaugh provide a road plan showing how the current route 455 can go off the road and crash into the underbrush of misunderstanding," Justice White started out reading. He looked up at Jake. "A bit purple, Jake boy?" He'd never referred to him in that collegial informality, but Jake liked that he did. The Justice kept reading what Jake had written for him.

"If you recall, 2400 law professors signed a public letter stating that Kavanaugh lacked judicial character and should not be confirmed. Statistically—based on recent court cases—over 20 percent of these professors on that list are likely to argue a case—any case, many cases, any subject—before the Supreme Court. How could Kavanaugh *not* be biased against them? Depending on the case, I could write the recusal petition in cases where they, or other 'left-wing Clinton operatives' were before the Court. His own words! I could go on and on—but you see my point. Kavanaugh could be knocked off the Court on most of its controversial cases on the basis of that transcript alone. Those who didn't want Kavanaugh on the Supreme Court might get their way, via the backdoor of recusals."

Justice White smiled when he read that passage. "Cute, Jake. I have to tone it down, but go to the hearing records and be sure to use specific quotes that actually were part of those hearings. No paraphrasing. We must get it completely factual. And check about the Catholic Church connections, Kavanaugh's and others', on the abortion issue. And Congress. I'll never forget the awful exchange between Kavanaugh and Sen. Klobochar at his confirmation questioning about blacking out from over drinking.

Jake returned to his anecdotal research while the Justice wrote what only he could write. This was more fun than Jake had had at work since arriving months ago. He was a veteran now, not a rookie. His time at the Court seemed like it had been happening forever. Had he ever been in another life?

Justice White combined his personal experiences, and those of other Justices, with Jake's research to make his point about 455's bias and prejudice language. His draft was good.

"What do those words—*bias, prejudice*—mean? No Justice will be quoted making racist or sexist or anti-religious remarks, even in this time of internet recordings and pictures. That's an easy one. But all of us have well-known views about all the hot-button issues. We can predict most Justices' votes because their historic views suggest where they stand. So, we all then start out biased and prejudiced—if those words are taken in their ordinary meaning."

"And what about review of recusal demands?" Jake's draft for the Justice continued. "How can it make sense to the public that we alone decide claims made against us? Our decisions are final. Sounds like some authoritative, un-American regime, doesn't it?

We may be right or wrong in our responses, but how can we be the final word when we are appropriately under scrutiny? What about *the appearance of justice*, if not justice itself? Recall the late Associate Justice Robert H. Jackson's perceptive remark, 'We are not final because we are infallible, but we are infallible only because we are final.'"

That last remark might generate applause, White pondered, so he would stop for a moment, to let the point be emphasized by such a reaction when he later delivered it.

Jake and Justice White worked in chambers whenever time allowed, editing the speech until they had to leave the Court for Union Station. Ms. Friedman said she'd be on call if last-minute changes were necessary. People in the office knew what was up, but they did not know the embargoed words or message the Justice would deliver. The invited press would all come to hear a visiting Supreme Court Justice. NYU's auditorium would be packed.

For the first time, Jake and Sydney were not together for several days, and rarely spoke. Sydney knew what he was up to; she was a bit jealous of his new extra-clerk role. Jake called as he and Justice White were leaving for Union Station.

"Goin' now, babe. I'll tell you about it tomorrow. I'm excited."

chapter 14

Fireworks, at Christmas?

Sydney and Jake knew in their minds they had to publicize and formalize their new partnership. But the convention open to most people wasn't available to them.

Often when they were together, Sydney and Jake talked about their parents meeting each other so the announcement of their engagement could be made to them jointly. Sydney seemed diffident about such a family conference. Jake pushed the idea after their future partnership was clear to them.

"Why don't we get our families together?" he suggested. "Mine are asking questions about me, us."

Sydney responded, "Mine don't know much about us, and frankly, I don't want them to."

Jake looked hurt.

"Jakey, you have an old-fashioned family, and you are their only son, the Jewish prince. My sister, Val, and I barely know each other. Never really lived together. I come from a pseudo 'Mayflowery' family who see themselves as elite, even though they aren't, really. Their church and club friends are their entire inner circle. Between you and me, they are racist, right-wing, and sorry to add, probably—no, definitely—anti-Semitic, even though they don't know any Jewish people up close and real. They are jealous of your people's successes without their people's help. I don't foresee a sweet family meeting as you do."

They made separate Christmas travel plans so Sydney could be alone with her family, when she would attempt to surface the Jake matter. Jake spent a long weekend with his family but returned early to Washington, where he would catch up with (he'd never get ahead of) his work at the Court.

Sydney returned to Washington after Christmas so they could have a few private days and nights together and share New Year's Eve. Ann was having a small dinner party at their apartment. They arrived to help her set up but excused themselves before midnight to watch the public celebration on the Mall from the rooftop of Jake's condo, which had a good view of the annual event that concluded with spectacular fireworks. Then they returned to Jake's apartment, and nightcaps were poured. They danced to Jake's classic Sinatra recordings. Their loving sleep that night contrasted with their recent empty separation. It was a very private, very personal, very intimate time together.

They shared breakfast that Sydney cooked after her late-morning run, and they talked about Jake's quiet, brief holiday with his family in New Jersey, and her intense and hurtful one in San Diego. Her parents had met there when her father was stationed during the Vietnam era at the local navy base. The perfect weather and her mother's pressure to stay where she had grown up prevailed. They spent holidays at Carmel, where they'd go for golfing and a party at their club. Sydney had wanted no part of that life, as they had discussed earlier. She'd called Jake. They'd agreed, happily, to meet in DC the next day, where he was working alone.

After breakfast and cleaning up dishes, they decided to have a long walk down Pennsylvania Avenue past the Canadian Embassy, the National Art Galleries, and the glass Botanical Gardens to sober up in the chilly but sunny late morning; then they would go to their separate chambers and turn on their minds again.

They surely sobered up from their mellow mood when Sydney told Jake how ugly their Christmas dinner had been. She'd let on that she and he were in love and serious about it.

"Mom, Dad, I want to tell you about a man I've met, another clerk on the Court, and have gotten serious with. Jake Lehman; he's from New Jersey and . . ."

Her mother had interrupted in her cold, impersonal way. "You had to bring up this subject during this rare time we are together, and just back from church, to boot. Thank you very much Sydney for your timing and consideration for your father and me," her mother had chided.

"Val was in Seattle with her husband's family. Mom and I fought. Dad was quiet, wanted no part of the negotiation. Then stony silence embraced the room. It went downhill from that high point," Sydney sighed. "Maybe I should go and teach at Rutgers. Your family is so nice."

"No," Jake said. "You belong at Stanford, but I appreciate your warm feelings about my small and happy family. It pays to be an only child. I thought these dumb questions about marriage ended years ago," he mused.

"Me, too," Sydney added. "For God's sake, families now argue about their kids marrying someone of another race, or the same sex. My family is back in the 1950s."

Sydney and Jake agreed on all the fundamentals like personal values, but on politics, not so much, and they approached contentious legal issues from different directions. Classic millennials, their views were not doctrinaire, Left or Right. Like the Justices they worked for, they agreed on about 80 percent of the issues in cases they worked on at the Court. Over dinners and informal chats, they saw that they were both conservative about fiscal matters—balancing the budget and fairer tax laws. They were on the same side of most social issues that were before the Court—equitable immigration reform and social services for folks who needed them. But they argued about moderate affirmative action (Jake was more conservative) and women's rights (Sydney naturally had a level of passion about this that Jake didn't share). On some few issues, they followed libertarian positions—legalizing marijuana, for example. Their debates were substantive, not personal, and never affected the deep relationship they had developed as lovers. They rather enjoyed these civilized and erudite discussions.

On life questions, Sydney had settled on an academic career; Jake wanted to do trial work. Like other millennials, they focused on their careers before considering marriage. Eventually, whenever that was, they both wanted two children, one of each sex, they agreed. Sydney wanted a tight family like Jake's, the kind she regretted missing out on in her own childhood. They'd make their own family, and the marital contract terms would evolve easily, they agreed.

chapter 15

The Lecture

Professor Leibowitz was able to persuade the dean to host Justice White's lecture. It wasn't a difficult task, as having a Supreme Court Justice—one with an NYU past—would bring out a large crowd and be good PR for the school. The dean was a master at law school promotion, and with the cooperation of the university's public relations department, invitations went out to major news outlets, law school funders, the faculty and student body, and other New York City pooh-bahs and illustrious public figures. The large auditorium was reserved, and the film department was alerted to prepare to record the Justice's talk.

The practice of clerks writing judicial decisions was common at the Court. Some judges, like the late William O. Douglas, insisted on writing their own opinions and using clerks for specific research assignments. Some merely edited their clerks' work and put their names on the drafts that were circulated by their colleagues to affirm or dissent. Justice White's practice was to use the clerks for research, preferring to write his own words for posterity. Clerks might draft a speech for him, but never an opinion. This speech, though, would be special, all involved hoped.

"Jake," Justice White had suggested as he prepared his speech, "I'd like to see some research that I think would help me make an important point. But I need to be sure my impressions and thesis are right."

"Which would be ...?" Jake asked.

"Which would be—I need data to demonstrate that, despite a distinguished record teaching constitutional law at Yale Law School and serving honorably as Solicitor General, Bork was treated at his confirmation hearing in the most hostile fashion. We even use the term 'Borked' now to describe a candidate being treated terribly by posturing politicians.

"That experience created a new period—one we're still in—when the Court has been politicized as never before, where controversial but competent candidates are coached to testify like it was some NOH play, and dissemble about their positions—'I'm just an umpire,' they now say, as if we're like traffic lights, not thinkers. We all must appear not to have biases and prejudices so we can survive the process, sometimes barely so. What kind of moral authority does a Justice bring to the Supreme Court after a contentious televised Senate hearing, and a 52-48 vote like Clarence Thomas and Brett Kavanaugh?"

He concluded, "Our first Chief Justice, John Marshall, is known for his opinion in the historic Marbury v. Madison on the question of judicial review. But that memorable case also set the lax standards for recusal we still are dealing with today."

"I'll check out the thesis, boss. Interesting idea."

Jake headed to the library, and did find some relevant history that would make it into Justice White's speech at NYU.

On the afternoon of the lecture, Justice White and Jake took the three-hour train ride to Penn Station, New York City, from Union Station, DC. A small welcome dinner was held in the law school's special occasions dining room, where select pictures of past deans lined the walls and bright conversation was the menu for this select group. Justice White left early and was escorted by the dean to the auditorium, where he would begin at 7:30.

Justice White's talk was entitled "Justice and the Appearance of Justice." He had improved and refined Jake's draft, and it contained his own passions on these subjects, ideas that Jake couldn't have known. Jake would always keep a copy of that speech in his memorabilia file.

The Justice began by telling the packed house, "The American public deserves courts—especially the Supreme Court—that are fair, just, and as apolitical as possible. All the more so at this divisive and contentious time when the country seemed to not be a *United* States." He alluded to an earlier administration and his days working in the Senate for then-senator, now President Treynor. "Politics was politics in those days. It was partisan. But it wasn't hateful, and common causes were not rare." He prayed that the country would find a new way to govern itself, and called upon everyone there, "students who are our future, faculty who are our educators, media who are our watchdogs—to participate in this reform."

As a judge who could not be involved in public campaigns, he asked himself what his contribution might be. Tonight, he wanted to offer a discreet suggestion that would affect him and his Court. He went on:

"You may know that the Supreme Court has a rule that permits Justices to be challenged to recuse themselves in cases of conflicts of interest, or where bias or prejudice exists. It is easy to agree with such an obvious requirement for the executive branch, the legislative branch, and especially the judiciary. I have no argument about that. But I do challenge our unique practice at the Supreme Court of allowing us, the Justices ourselves, to decide whether or not to recuse ourselves when challenged, and that there is no appeal of our conclusion, nor adequate public consideration of it."

Justice White offered examples of his point, using the Sandra Day O'Connor story as Exhibit One. He apologized for criticizing a former judge but added that he could offer no better example of the point he wished to make, and as the Justice was deceased, he offered his remarks as history. He had no animus toward the late Justice, whom he personally admired.

Justice White had done his homework and presented data that he had gathered about recusal practices in the federal court system. Judges were supposed to balance the constitutional need to protect judicial independence with the need to demonstrate to the public that there was no "inside self-protectionism." Referring to these standards, he found in Court studies that the federal court of appeals handled about sixty-thousand cases a year, from which eighty cases are accepted by the Court for its decision—which was problematic. That was the interesting data Jake had dug up from Court records.

Most demands for recusal were by prisoners and litigants, and most were dismissed. In addition, he noted the "duty to sit" doctrine, which dictated that judges cannot simply decide to disqualify themselves without a law requiring them to do so. "Some states permit peremptory challenges, where judges have no discretion," he told the audience.

"The problem is that the few high-visibility cases raise questions in the public's mind and create an image of justice that may not be reflective of the day-to-day work we do." He pointed that "we were unanimous in about half our cases last year. eighty cases are accepted by the Court for its decision"

Then he offered his own case as a hypothetical, as if he had never dealt with it before, hoping he never would have to.

proposal, one I offer tonight for independent consideration. This is not exclusively a judicial issue, but one of public policy. Before I came here this evening, I discussed my idea with the Chief Justice, who as you know has sundry administrative responsibilities regarding court business. I am pleased to say he endorsed my idea and is at work with the Administrative Office of the Court to develop, after it is assessed by interested experts, a new recusal rule. I hope you will follow this matter when it becomes public. I'll use one anecdote from my experience to make the point, though my intent is to suggest a better way to deal with *all* recusal claims in the future."

Then, in an offhand, incidental aside, the Justice explained the dilemma he had struggled with recently, leaving out details that had to remain confidential but subtly evoking them to make his larger point.

"There is a case that could potentially arise in our court—of course, I can't disclose it now. I only offer it as an example we Justices all face, regularly, reluctantly. Most of you know that I worked for President Treynor when he was a New York senator, as his legislative assistant. We had a cordial, professional relationship then, and we do now. But when I read about one incident that might come before the Court—one involving issues I have written about and care deeply about—I looked at the guiding statute, 455, and discovered that it provided me with inadequate guidance. Worse, it appeared to cover *any* subject I or my colleagues on the Court might be called upon to adjudicate.

"We all have strong opinions about all issues coming before the Court—how could we not? Should we then recuse ourselves because we all have personal, religious, and historical viewpoints about these issues? Isn't it good that we do? Dealing with abstractions is of little use."

Then White moved into delicate waters, though his clerks had advised against it, because he thought the example would make sense to all people—Republicans, Democrats, liberals, or conservatives.

"If I were called upon to decide a case that affected our President, intellectually, politically, personally, must I step aside because it would *look* injudicious not to? Every Justice was appointed by some president to whom he or she would be eternally grateful. But, history has shown, not always, that this conclusion is not inevitable. President Eisenhower is reported to have said appointing Earl Warren as Chief Justice was his biggest disappointment as president." White never mentioned the issues in his recent case, but some listeners might have guessed he referred to the notorious Dawson case.

"I concluded that I would be—if such a case arose—in an impossible situation. What, I thought, if there was an impartial umpire, an ombudsman of sorts, to whom I would be able to pass on the recusal question? I would agree to abide by his or her ruling, whether I concurred with it or not. The complaint and the ruling would be decisive, and public. We all would be spared the unnecessary and improvident and important precedent of *appearing* to be wrong, whether we might or might not be. The integrity of our high court requires it."

The audience's response was most positive. Students and faculty members stood and applauded long and loud when he concluded, and many attendees approached him before he could leave the stage to compliment him on his idea. The student and faculty leaders of the law journal asked for permission to print

his remarks in its next issue, with his editing, possibly with concurring or dissenting articles on the point that deserved to be
aired. Justice White agreed.

Professor Leibowitz came up and hugged him, and they
exchanged a private smile. Media attendees kept him late asking
questions and seeking copies of his talk. The New York City
papers highlighted his remarks the next day under headlines
like: "Supreme Court Justice Calls for Fairer Recusal Procedures
at the Court." The solution Leibowitz had suggested worked.

chapter 16

From Mentor to Friend

Judge White was elated at the public's reception to his talk. After the evening's formalities ended, he pushed back their original early-morning departure time to Washington, insisting on taking Meyer and Jake to a hearty celebratory brunch at Irv's, a favorite deli in the NYU neighborhood where they had spent the night. They met at ten and ate what Meyer called "soul food"—bagels and lox, mountainous pastrami and corned beef sandwiches (Meyer took home half of his), and Dr. Brown's Cel-Ray Tonic, culinary exotica one could only find in New York City, rarely in Washington. They talked more about their prior evening and reveled in Justice White's execution of Meyer's idea.

When the Justice and Jake left for the one o'clock train to DC, Meyer hugged them both and walked off smiling. They hailed a cab to Penn Station and barely got there in time to get them home before dinnertime. Jake felt he had become part of a remarkable three-generation friendship of intellectuals.

The ride home provided a rare few hours when Jake and Justice White chatted informally, almost as equal colleagues, which would never have happened in ordinary circumstances. They dissected the Justice's talk, agreeing that they had made all the points in their joint creative process writing together, remembering the comments made to the Justice by some of the attending press, wondering if the continuing coverage of the talk would be as successful as they'd deemed the event.

Then, their formal guards down, Jake asked, "Justice White, can I ask you a question about the censorship subject?"

"Of course. It is a subject I have written about, as you know."

"I've known, since law school Constitutional Law 101, that prior restraint goes back to Near v. Minnesota in 1931 and has been followed, and in fact expanded, since then. I'm curious to know your thoughts about the general policy that the remedy for free discussion that is protected by the First Amendment in federal cases and the Fourteenth in those involving states is limited to libel law if the printed matter is false, not prior restraint."

"You have a problem with that principle?" White asked.

"Not at all," Jake answered. "But haven't things changed in modern times, where digital language on the internet can be so prejudicial and anonymous that relief by suing for libel is an unlikely remedy? As a matter of public policy, it could be a dangerous tool in the hands of irresponsible internet users."

"There are exceptions to the rule, as you know . . . obscenity, national security," White said, "but even in those situations my view has been that the greater value is open and free discussion. Read Justice Black's concurring opinion in *New York Times* v. United States. It is eloquent. He quoted James Madison: 'The press is to serve the governed, not the governors.'"

Jake hesitated, then said, "I know that case. It involved the Pentagon Paper articles in the *Washington Post* and *New York Times* critical of the Vietnam War. Professor Bickel argued for the *Times,* and Solicitor General Erwin Griswold argued for the government. Yale v. Harvard. It must have been a great case to hear argued."

"Yes," White interrupted, "and years later Griswold wrote an op-ed in the *Post* saying there really was no national security issue in that case, only the government wanting to hide its bad policies

... exactly what prior-restraint critics believe is the rationale for that law. It was a long way from the Pentagon Papers," Justice White remarked, smiling, "to the Dawson tell-all."

Their conversation went on informally as their train passed Philadelphia and Wilmington, until they were closer to home. Jake loved the repartee, realized that his Justice was a scholar who surely knew his Constitution. No experience in law school matched their few hours chatting about censorship, its dramatic history, its literary lessons in famous cases like restraining Joyce's *Ulysses* and Henry Miller's erotic novels. Jake was more conservative than the Justice when he wasn't writing what the Justice wanted written in his name, much as he and Sydney differed, always engagingly and intellectually stimulatingly.

As their train arrived at Union Station and they gathered their papers and other overnight belongings, Justice White wrapped his arm around Jake's shoulder, graciously saying, "You have a good and critical mind, Jake. Keep questioning me on these important issues, me and everyone." As they left the train and hurried through the vast vestibule, Justice White called a Lyft to avoid the line in front of the station and went home, while Jake briskly walked back to the Court half a dozen blocks away to catch up on the day in the office, and hopefully to see Sydney, who would still be there.

Jake was high on the evolving relationship between him and his boss and wanted to tell her about his adventure in the big leagues of law.

chapter 17

The Truce

No one was surprised when the Justice's chambers received a call the next day from Eric Yancy. The Conservative Society had discussed the *New York Times*, *Wall Street Journal*, and *Washington Post* stories about Justice White's NYU speech and proposal. Eric made an appointment through Ms. Friedman to meet with Jake at the end of the day. "Tell him I owe him a drink. See him at Scales at seven."

Ms. Friedman told Jake after his return in the late afternoon. Jake wasn't surprised, but he was wary.

They met early that evening as planned. Eric was at a quiet booth, sitting alone, and Jake joined him.

"Hey, how's it going?" Jake slid into the booth, where a pitcher of beer and two glasses waited.

"You know why I'm here," Eric replied.

"I can guess," Jake replied.

"I think we both can come out of this contretemps all right," Eric offered.

"How's that?" Jake was surprised. He'd been expecting an argument.

"We sent the letter to open the question. You now can send us your *belated* response, enclosing Justice White's talk, and call on us to endorse your idea. If we do, and the ACLU too, as I would expect them to, you will have bipartisan endorsements, and your law alma mater's review gets some limelight. Everyone wins."

"And your group comes out looking like you generated the idea about reform of the recusal law. You don't get what you were after if these cases never get to the Supreme Court, and there's no guarantee they will, but if you go public with your so-called endorsement, pushing for recusal reform and acting like you started the conversation, to your supporters you'd look like influential statesmen. You guys sure are good poker players. If the censorship or the pardon issue ever do come to the Court, and White isn't recused, you guys lose his vote against censorship, and if it arises, which we doubt, on unrestricted pardons, you lose his vote, but you knew that the whole time."

"Hey, what can I say?" Eric concluded, smiling, picking up the drinks bill and rising to leave. "We should work together again when our interests are the same." He winked.

chapter 18

Someone from the Past

Leo Tolstoy once wrote that all stories follow two basic themes—a person goes on a journey or a stranger comes to town. That second theme was part of Sydney's and Jake's love story, too. Just when they had both become comfortable with their clerk lives and their new city and each other, they had a problem.

Jake and Sydney were looking forward to a private, indulgent night together after a busy and stressful few weeks. Ann had an out-of-town guest, so Sydney offered her bed so Ann's friend wouldn't have to sleep on the couch. That was their signal . . . whenever they could get away from their offices. That Saturday, they would spend the night together at Jake's condo. Sydney had made her gumbo specialty the Sunday before and brought it to Jake's place. "Keep this in your freezer until next Saturday, and pick up one of your special wines, and you can get me drunk."

"A deal." Jake smiled in anticipation. "Maybe our married colleagues don't have it so bad," he added.

"Right," Sydney said, "wouldn't it be fun to come home from ten hours at the Court and deal with the latest strep throat one of the kids has?"

Jake didn't bother to parry her sarcasm. He was already busy thinking about Saturday night alone with her for a romantic evening.

They both got to the Court even earlier than usual so they could have a whole evening to squander amid candlelight and slow, low Brubeck. They managed to hurry through deadline assignments so they could leave together by six o'clock.

Jake had hired the condo cleanup crew to bring his digs up to Sydney's standards earlier that day, and together they picked up flowers on their way home.

"Jake, did you rent a new apartment?" Sydney asked as they entered his unusually tidy quarters. Jake smiled and filled a large, glass pitcher with bright-colored cosmos, his favorite. Sydney went straight to the kitchen to address her now mostly unfrozen gumbo, which Jake had remembered to defrost before leaving for work.

Each of them rushed through changing into comfortable clothes and refreshing in Jake's tiny bathroom.

Jake set the table and clicked on Pandora for one of their favorite Beegie Adair piano selections, while Sydney began cooking dinner.

The mood was made for love.

But it didn't last long.

"Remember that chamber music thing we were going to go to with Ann and some of the gang next week?" Sydney asked.

"Yeah, what about it? Not my favorite thing to do on a free night when we could be doing this," he called from the other room.

Sydney came to him, wiping her cooking hands, acting nonchalant. "Turns out I may not have to drag you there after all. Remember my old boyfriend, Ed Vector? He's an engineer now in Portland. His company is sending him to a conference on government contracting at the Building Museum that night, and he called to ask me if we could have dinner and catch up."

"We?" Jake asked, in an unusually weak, questioning voice.

"Sure, you can come if you want to, " Sydney responded, sensing Jake's hesitance. "But no need to if you don't want to," she offered. "I doubted you'd want to sit in on me catching up with a friend from my past."

Jake sighed.

"What's the matter, Jake? You aren't mad that he and I are still long-distance friends, I hope."

"No, why would I be?"

"I give up, why would you?" Now Sydney dropped being diplomatic and empathetic and changed her mood, sitting down on the couch after pouring a glass of the wine Jake had left breathing for their breathless night ahead. Sydney's tone became formal. "What's wrong? I told you about Ed when we first became us, remember? We have remained long-distance friends since we both left high school, and send each other year-end gossip about our lives. He knows about you and me."

"Yeah? What does he know?"

"This is silly, beneath you, Jake. Are you suggesting that I'm going behind your back, getting back with an old flame?"

"I didn't suggest anything. You just did," a petulant Jake snarled back.

"Well this is turning into some fine evening, Mr. Lehman."

"So it's Mr. Lehman, now."

"Geez, Jake, I can't believe this. What are you implying, worrying about?"

"Forget it."

"No, I won't forget it now and have our romantic dinner after this tense scene."

"So you're walking out on it, me, now?"

"That what you want?"

"No, but it seems it's what you want."

With that, Sydney stood, walked to the other room, put on her coat, and reached for the front door.

"Sydney, come back. Don't leave like this. I am jealous, I suppose. Don't leave."

"Sorry, dearie, I need some fresh air." She slammed the door as she left.

Now Jake was confused, upset, contrite. He went straight to Mr. Bourbon and poured himself a neat splash and drank it fast, moving around the room, distraught. Where would she go, he wondered to himself, thinking about running after her, apologizing, bringing the evening back to its intended purpose. But he had no idea where she'd gone. His call to her went straight to voicemail, so he called Ann to ask if she was there.

"I thought she was with you. Is something wrong, Jake?"

"No, don't worry. Just a little mix-up. If you hear from her, tell her I'm waiting at my apartment."

Now Jake was disconcerted and remorseful. *What have I done? What am I doing?* he wondered.

While Jake was attempting to track her down, Sydney was sitting at a back booth, alone at Scales, which was half empty at that time between drinks after work and before dinner. She was sipping a scotch on the rocks, a stronger drink than her usual. Pouting. Trying to figure out what exactly was happening.

She was half flattered Jake would be jealous of her old friend, half annoyed that he was so unsure of what she was sure they had between themselves. Then the barkeep came up to her, saying, "You Sydney?"

"Yes," she replied, confused, drawn back to earth.

"Stay here," he replied. "There's a guy on the phone asking if you were here. Okay for me to tell him you are?"

"If his name is Jake, I guess so."

Within minutes, Jake burst into the quiet barroom, looked around, and spotting Sydney, came to her booth, silent, and sat down.

Neither said a word. Then Jake asked, "What are you doing? That doesn't look like white wine."

Sydney didn't answer, just looked down and kept quiet.

Jake jumped in. "Sydney, I'm sorry to have acted like a jealous high-school kid whose girlfriend ran off."

"With the football star?" Sydney asked, with a half-smile.

"Yeah, I don't know what got into me. The idea of you out with a man, any man, especially one you had a relationship with . . . it scared me. I'm sorry." He ran a hand through his hair and exhaled before continuing. "You and Ed should have your dinner together without me just sitting there nodding. Talk about whatever you want to talk about. Message me when you get to coffee, and I'll come pick you up, meet Ed, take you home."

"That would be nice. Thank you, Jakey."

"Do we have to invite him to our wedding?" Jake grinned.

Sydney moved her hand across the table, holding Jake's. "I should have handled it in not-so-offhand a way, so I'm sorry too. You must understand I am a total person in what I do with my life. I am totally with you. But I'll always be a special friend of Ed's. He's engaged, you should know, and we are just old, special friends catching up."

"I know. I know," Jake whispered. "I love you so much. Please forgive me. Come back to me."

"You're just after my gumbo, buddy. I know. Don't fake it."

They slid together out of the booth, hugged, and walked off, looking forward to the evening they had planned and lost, temporarily.

chapter 19

Death of a Book

The Dawson book was still out there, despite the injunction, which was on appeal. The problem remained. Then, sub rosa, behind-the-scenes justice—Washington style—took over.

At first, the public didn't notice. All of a sudden, *Deserted*, the Dawson book, evaporated. The publisher stripped it from its seasonal catalogs. Distributors didn't have books, so bookstore orders went unfulfilled. Friends of Dawson reported that they couldn't find or order her book, wherever they lived. Reviews stopped. *Sixty Minutes* canceled its scheduled interview. Dawson was outraged. The scandal sheets moved on to the next movie star divorce or charges of sexual abuse against a schoolteacher or business mogul.

How that literary death came to happen eventually became public—sort of—after Dawson and her attorney challenged her publisher, Harrow House, and were stonewalled. "Our decision has been made to publish no more," the prim publisher explained—no reason was offered. No explanation.

When Dawson found journalists who would look into her sudden banishment, they too hit a stone wall of silence. Eventually, the secret came out—they always do in stories of Washington intrigue. Like a weed that manages to push through a crack in a cement sidewalk, a Washington political secret eventually comes out, unofficially.

The Dawson blackball eventually found its way into the public domain. No one really knew how, but a version of the true story was told in a small, alternative DC newspaper. The rumor was that the renowned "fixer" lawyer, Beauford "Beau" Clark—close to President Treynor—and a veteran hardball Republican political powerhouse met privately with each other. That was never proven, but the anonymous story was vetted by the local paper's lawyers before it was published. Apparently, the New York City editor was told—by Beau through indirect threats—that continued publication of the Dawson book would be so offensive to the President's supporters that it might be that important Washington celebrity books would cease coming their way. He told the publisher, who was aghast at the hardball thrown at their company's head, but after lunch, and conversations with his board, one of whom seemed to know about the threat and counseled that this was not "a hill worth dying on" for their company, the decision was made to lose the battle with Beau et al., and not lose the long-term, very profitable Washington book business.

Shock about the questions of impact on the First Amendment this incident raised disappeared in a few days, and no one spoke of it after. No one knew who had done what to make this unheard-of "book burning" happen. The story ended with confusion in some quarters as the only repercussions.

The President never spoke of it. Ms. Dawson was bereft. The scandal story ended, slowly but completely.

Only the President and Washington insider attorney Beauford "Beau" Clark knew of the private conversation they'd had as they left for their off-again, on-again regular poker game with major Washington movers and shakers. The President wanted his friend, the Justice, left out of the contretemps. The malicious Dawson charges had embarrassed President Treynor and worried political operatives who were gearing up for the midterm elections. Beau Clark's reputation preceded him on all his private missions. When he was occasionally rebuffed, consequences followed—untraceable, but undebatable.

The inside story insinuated that Beau had met in New York City with the head of Harrow House Publications to discuss *Deserted*. As they sat in his capacious office, the publisher's private secretary interrupted to say there was an important call from the White House for Mr. Clark. Clark excused himself, remarking as he left to accept the call, "I apologize. I assure you this call has nothing to do with our conversation."

The publisher got the point. Clark returned a few minutes later, saying as he sat down before him, "Now let's talk about the matter of our client's concern." Certain Washington lawyers— Beau especially—billed exceedingly generously for "resolving" matters such as this hour-long conversation. The top negotiators were charging $1,000 an hour for corporate work. "Special assignments" like Beau's might net him a $50,000 retainer from a special interest group. It paid for a lot of Beau's pro bono work for the Republican party and its spin-off PACs.

Justice White's recusal in the censorship case had become moot. And without an indictment of the President—none came—so was any issue of Treynor's having to pardon himself. But Justice White was not through with his intention to reform the recusal law.

chapter 20

Sharing Intimacies

As summer receded and October got closer, the Court was busier than ever. The different Justices shared assigned opinions they drafted and circulated. They lobbied their colleagues to join their drafts of majority opinions, concurring opinions, and dissents that were circulated daily. The clerks were overworked just keeping up with the flow. Lights were on in the chambers and the libraries past midnight. Staff were running around, more than usual. Secretaries, computers, and the sound of printers spitting out reams of paper were all in action.

Jake and Sydney rarely saw one another, except incidentally when their Justices conferred on matters of mutual Court interest. The Chief Justice had work beyond what the Associate Justices had, along with his work on cases about to be announced, so Sydney was exhausted as that last week in September neared its end. Without any formal announcement, it was clear that the Chief relied especially on Sydney, and their relationship was mutually respectful.

Her office phone rang early one evening, and Jake was on the line asking, "How are you managing?"

"I can't talk now. What's up?"

"I have a brainstorm," he rattled off quickly. "When we get done Saturday, let's rent a car and get away from here. We've never seen the Skyline Drive and the Blue Ridge Mountains. Why don't we go someplace, stay overnight? It's only seventy-five miles. We could come back on Sunday?"

"OK, great idea," Sydney responded and hung up the phone. Jake didn't take her brusqueness personally. He knew she was as overworked as he and the others, more if that was possible.

If Jake was the social-idea half of the couple, Sydney was Ms. Execution. Before Saturday arrived, she had asked Ann to borrow her old red Mini Cooper for the day, and Ann had agreed. She made an online reservation for two at the Shenandoah Lodge, a sprawling, old-fashioned railroad hotel, surrounded with rustic cabins for privacy. It sat in the middle of the wooded, winding, leaf-changing trails that visitors could walk before returning to their cottage's warm, cozy fireplace. They could dine at the lodge in elegance and sleep alone in their cabin in a cushy bed. It would be the tonic they both needed. She even reserved a candlelit table for two for a late dinner Saturday night after they had walked the trails nearby.

They finished their work in the afternoon, met at the car, and drove the hour-and-a-half route to the wooded Virginia mountain site. As soon as they were out of Washington, they passed vineyards and saw spectacular stone fences marking off scenic meadows. Washington was fading, just as they'd hoped.

They arrived at the curving entrance of the lodge, courtesy of Waze, checked in at the main desk, left the car and overnight bags as it was getting late in the afternoon, and took off on a four-mile walk along the trails in the national park. As if central casting had set the scene, after they had gone deeper into the forest surrounding the trail, Sydney stopped. "Jake, look!" A large-antlered stag was fifty yards away, standing still, staring at them. It was a scene they would always remember.

After their colorful, quiet walk, they returned to find their bags had been set in the cabin, the deck of which had a spectacular view of the changing foliage. A crackling fire was going in their fireplace. It was Shangri-La. They showered, dressed, and arrived at dinner at the nearby lodge by eight. They splurged—venison for Jake, Dover sole for Sydney, and a bottle of gorgeous Medoc, and they shared one indulgent Grand Marnier soufflé. Their dinner wasn't over until 10:30, when they sat before the smoky fireplace alone in the old-fashioned, wood-paneled bar, holding hands as they dreamily sipped Armagnac from bulging snifters.

That night, cuddled in a king-sized, linen-sheeted, copiously pillowed bed, loopy from their rich and alcoholic dinner, their conversation entered a place of intimacy that prior times together they had never approached. They were away from their common places and schedules for the first time. Formalities disappeared. Languorous engagement gave way to very private thoughts they had never explored or expressed out loud before, to themselves or anyone.

"Jake," Sydney asked, "do you like making love to me as much as I do with you?"

"Umm," he responded sleepily, surprised at her very personal question. "When I first saw you, I was intimidated, thought you might be an overachieving ice queen. Who knew you were such a hot tamale?"

Sydney poked him at that remark but didn't let the conversation lapse. "When we first met, I thought you were a sweet, unsure nerd, but cute. Not what you turned out to be. Take off your glasses, put aside your earnest demeanor, and you become a different man. No longer my first impression as Clark Kent, but suddenly 'Super Guy'!"

"And what is that?"

"Warm, gentle, caring, modest, but very smart"—she laughed easily—"and horny."

Jake laughed. They embraced. Conversation stopped. The setting was fulfilling its romantic potential. They cuddled together into an enduring, slow, very loving embrace, and after a sudden rush of intimacy, they soon fell asleep, depleted but in a deep, very personal love.

A few hours before dawn, Sydney woke, reached over, and touched Jake's back. He groaned, waking, and her touch circled and went lower. Groggy, Jake rolled toward her. "You are a hot one, aren't you?" Conversation stopped and they touched, and kissed, and made love again. This time they came together in an intimate way they hadn't before and fell back asleep, cuddled together, disheveled, unconscious. Sydney had been the creative explorer; Jake the ardent follower.

Out of habit, Sydney awoke first and quietly dressed and went off on her run. When she returned, she heard the shower, saw the empty bed, slipped out of her running clothes, and surprised Jake, who turned in the shower as she entered, and they embraced. "We have to do this again next week," he whispered in her ear.

"Yeah, I knew how you'd love the trees turning color." Then she gasped as Jake engulfed her, under the rain of their hot shower.

Their personal musings continued over a late country breakfast. "What about the religion thing?" Jake asked, not out of the blue after Sydney's recent report about her mother. Their future was taking over their past.

"What about it?" she answered.

"Well, we're different. We—you at least—have an unhappy family. Will we confuse our children? Fight about having a Christmas tree? Does church interest you?"

"It does my family. And I like Sunday mornings when I do get to church, kind of punctuating my secular life, however briefly. I do—not often—go to an empty church . . . just to think about things. What about you?"

"I'm an emotional, cultural Jew—genuflect about Israel, fear anti-Semitism. Rarely go to Temple, though my parents do and hope I will too."

"Truth be told," Sydney remarked, "my mother and father talk a good Episcopalian, but they don't walk the walk. We've stopped discussing issues like women priests and gay marriage. We're in different worlds."

"Yeah," Jake answered. "Christianity is a neat idea. People should try it sometime."

Sydney laughed. "Will we fret over Palestine?" she queried.

"Probably," he grinned. "What about Bar Mitzvahs?" he asked.

"I don't know. What about them?" Sydney answered.

"Just so our son becomes a doctor." At this, they both laughed.

"We all go through life, until now, following—or running away from—our parents' habits. Then we reach a time where we have to decide for ourselves how to lead our lives, and their habits don't necessarily make sense to us, and our habits—ours— haven't yet developed."

That conversation went no place. There was no plan. Soon, they packed up, and after a short trail walk, left for their return trip to reality.

Their day away from A-type Washington was a reverie. Sunday had been a lazy day, mostly outdoors—hiking, talking, thinking only about each other. No court business was even considered.

During the slow, traffic-ridden drive back to Washington on Sunday, and in the throes of mellowness from their pre-departure hike on nearby trails, after their major brunch, they talked little. For a while, Sydney's head dropped as she dozed off. Even with her mouth slightly open and her slight, sibilant snore, when Jake looked over, she was beautiful. *If I can adore this lady in this private pose, it must be love. And I do*, he thought to himself.

They were in another place.

chapter 21

What about the Future?

Sydney and Jake agreed they had to attend the birthday party, dip-lomatically, for one of their fellow clerks—Emma Davis, whom she and Jake both liked. The party started late and was a bore. Drinks went on too long, and there was too much inside gossip about the Court's cases. When Sydney asked Jake if he was ready to go early, he jumped at the chance to leave. They both were hungry and easily decided to go to their favorite restaurant in Chinatown, Joe's Canton, which was close by and soon would close.

When they arrived shortly before 10 p.m., the cashier was closing up, and the dining room was empty but for two tables toward the back of the room crowded with kitchen employees and their families, who regularly met for late dinner after the customers were gone.

Suzy, the cashier, recognized Sydney and Jake, who were regular dim sum customers, and when they pleaded to come in—"Only for our favorite dumplings," Sydney said—they were quietly seated, the door was locked, and in a while, two straw baskets of their special steaming dumplings were brought to their isolated table by one of the kitchen staff, along with chopsticks and a teapot and two small cups.

The relaxed couple held hands, and gathered and consumed the magical dumplings with their chopsticks and special spoons, unconscious of the noisy clatter and loud conversations in Chinese coming from the back of the restaurant.

Out of the blue, Jake asked where things stood with her job offer from Stanford. Sydney looked down, hesitated, and replied reluctantly, "Jake, I'm conflicted. I want to take the position. I don't want to be a spinster going from one irresistible professional opportunity to the next until I'm too old to have a family. You don't know yet about the job in San Francisco you were offered, and I don't want to pressure you to take a job to please me."

"If I did, it would be to please *me*—more about being with you than having that job. There's other jobs I could have, as you know."

Sydney was quiet. Jake's sentimental remark touched her. "I guess it's priorities, for both of us," she offered. "What's the point? Job or marriage." She'd not used that word—*marriage*—before, even though it was implicit in all their agonizing conversations about the future.

Neither Sydney nor Jake had planned to have this heavy conversation at such an inappropriate time and place, though both had known it was going to happen sometime soon. In a few months, the Court would be concluding its summer recess, and all the clerks would be training their new replacements, preoccupied with job applications and offers, decisions about joining lucrative law firm offices or prestigious government and academic positions. But having opened the question, dropping it while they ate their impromptu dumplings, they returned to it after thanking Suzy and paying. They walked slowly home to Jake's apartment, a long walk away. Their routine was to go to Jake's apartment when they sensed (code for not saying it aloud) that it was an evening for romance and Sydney's roommate was home.

"Jake," Sydney began, taking his hand, "Palo Alto is about thirty-five miles from San Francisco, a forty-five-minute drive. Since I would only be teaching and going to meetings three days a week, and you'd be working long hours for your firm, if we lived in San Francisco, we could be together four of seven days a week *and* seven nights." She smiled at him and squeezed his hand at this last remark.

"I suppose," Jake admitted. "But first, I'm not sure it's Millerton-Roberts I'd want to go to if I decide to go the practice route. They're the biggest firm in town, pay the most for sure. I'm embarrassed how much I'd be making in my first job. San Francisco is a fun place, but I'm an East Coast guy. I'd be leaving all my past behind. I'd at least have the Giants." He'd obviously been thinking about this conversation, and in his orderly way had listed all the pros and cons. "The Solicitor General's Office is inquiring about my availability, and if I went there I'd be arguing before the Supreme Court. I know my family will be disappointed if I don't come back. 'New York City isn't far from New Jersey,' they keep lobbying."

"I know. I know. Maybe we should take a trip around the world for a year before we settle anywhere," Sydney lamented. "We've both been on a consuming merry-go-round to get to this point in our young lives. If we don't take time out, it will be all work, raising children, and all of a sudden we'll look up and be sixty-five . . ." She trailed off in mid-sentence, unsure where to go with that idea, and if she really meant it, when she knew she loved the idea of returning to the Stanford campus she adored.

"How much time 'til you have to tell them?" Jake asked.

"I don't have a time limit. No one—certainly no one my age and stage—says no to an offer of a professorship at Stanford Law School. They probably presume I will accept. I suppose I could drag my feet a short while. What about you? When do you think you will decide?"

By this time, they had reached Jake's apartment, entered, and continued their conversation as they eased out of their party clothes and relaxed on Jake's couch while he poured them each a neat bourbon. For a moment, it was quiet. Then Sydney sighed, "Jake, I don't want to talk. I want to make love to you." She turned, reaching out to him.

Given this option, and with no more that could be said about the future, Jake submitted to Sydney's sly, if evasive suggestion.

chapter 22

The Justice Addresses Congress

Now that Justice White had the public's attention and the cooperation of the Chief Justice, it seemed the reform of the hollow recusal laws might just happen. The Senate Judiciary Committee, which had oversight responsibilities for the federal courts, had seen the reaction to White's NYU speech as a cause to champion. Hearings were set. When White was asked to appear, he deferred to the Chief Justice, whose administrative duties defined him as the appropriate witness. The Chief, perhaps to assuage his colleague's frustrations with his reluctance to have any role in White's earlier dilemma, asked White to appear with him to present a united front.

When they arrived, the scene at Room 314-A of the Senate Russell Building hardly resembled Watergate, or even the charged scene of Silicon Valley executives before a packed house teeming with media. Only a few committee members attended, backed by a few of their young staff members. Guest seats were empty for the most part. A few press regulars stopped in only because the calendar indicated the Chief Justice would be in attendance; Dennis McCarthy came and stayed. This was how the business of government took place, day to day, and serious issues of public policy were managed, quietly and collegially.

The Chief spoke first—rank always counts. But he simply introduced the subject to follow and thanked the committee for its invitation. He told the members that "While the Judiciary and Supreme Court are jealous of its independent constitutional powers under Article III of our Constitution, we are also respectful of Congress's power under Article I to deal with 'the tribunals inferior to the Supreme Court.' The matter of recusal of Supreme Court Justices is not covered by the existing legislation governing the inferior courts. We address today, exclusively, the statutory procedure governing recusal in our Court, 28 USC 455. From time to time, our Court has been criticized about an individual Justice's application of 455. I believe that my administrative powers authorize me to regulate our application of it. But I believe it would be consistent with our requirement of independence to work collaboratively with Congress and arrive at a recusal policy more explicit than 455 is now, and a procedure assuring the appearance of justice.

"I turn to Justice White now to discuss this problem, and the solution we would offer to share with Congress. He has studied the problem and has spoken publicly and wisely about it. I turn to him now, at the Committee's will."

"Please continue, Justice White," the lackluster but cordial Oklahoma senator, Ted Harris, responded. "The committee welcomes you both and appreciates the collegial approach you have demonstrated."

Justice White shifted his chair closer to the microphone, greeted and thanked the Committee, and proceeded to make the pitch he (with Sydney and Jake's help) had written.

"Since my talk at NYU several weeks ago," he began, "I have received many messages from citizens, scholars, judges, and interested organizations, responding to my comments about the current Supreme Court recusal law. Most people agree with me that it is idiosyncratic and perverse that, of all people, we Justices decide claims about our biases and impartiality with only vague and no specific guidelines about what those imprecise words mean.

"Take what might seem at first a classic example of bias or partiality that might warrant a Justice being recused. After Thurgood Marshall was Solicitor General and then a Court of Appeals judge, he took the position that if a case he had worked on arose after he was appointed to the Supreme Court, he should always disqualify himself. He did so fifty-seven times in his first term. Some jokingly teased he was in quasi-retirement. More recently, my colleague Justice Elena Kagan often recuses herself—twenty-eight out of seventy-eight cases in one year— from voting or considering in cases arising from the time when she was Solicitor General and either oversaw or argued cases for the government. One could argue that she was overqualified to sit on those cases, and that her impressive history did not warrant her being paid *not* to deliberate or sit on all those cases. Even the revered first Chief Justice John Marshall, also a former Solicitor General, recused himself seventy-five times in his first term!

"Another problem is being steeped in the study of legal issues or having expertise on subjects, some have thought, as was the case with Felix Frankfurter, who came to the Supreme Court from a remarkable career teaching law school, that made him 'biased' or 'partial' because he had developed learned positions on subjects he taught and advocated for in courts and legislatures. One could also argue this very reason made him the perfect judge to sit as a Justice, because he knew more than other judges who hadn't studied a subject before the Court or known the law as Frankfurter did.

"The other question that can be raised is when a Justice recuses herself, as Sandra Day O'Connor did, in a case involving a company in which she had stock. Is that requirement always so clear? All Justices probably have stocks and bond portfolios, and may not even know what stocks they own. Do they all have to recuse themselves for their financial interests? In every case?

"What about a Justice like Louis Brandeis, whose brilliant career labeled him ideologically in a way other judges were not because their careers were not so visible, and the Senate knew little about him? Do we want only vanilla Justices who come to the Court for political reasons, without deep jurisprudential experience? Why wouldn't that experience make him or her *more* qualified?

"One could argue both positions," Justice White went on. "Concluding on opposite sides of these exemplary situations could be correct and judicious. The appearance of justice is important, but it also can be an empty phrase. It sounds correct, but it need not be so in fact. Justice Hugo Black had been in the Ku Klux Klan as a young Alabama lawyer and was appointed by Franklin D. Roosevelt specifically for shifting the Court in its positions at that time on national economic issues. He was confirmed by a vote of 63–16. He turned out—I would argue— to be a great and liberal Justice. President Eisenhower said he regretted appointing Earl Warren Chief Justice for political reasons when Warren turned out to be the very personification of the opposite point of view Eisenhower had presumed. Same with Justices Brennan and Souter, whose positions surprised the two presidents who appointed them. Do we want Justices who sign on in advance about their points of view, as is often the case in the recent history when the confirmation process in the Senate has often appeared more political than judicial? I always admired President Eisenhower and his influential attorney general, Herbert Brownell Jr., for appointing a few Democratic justices because the country needed bipartisanship on controversial matters likely to come before the Court in that era of civil rights conflicts and McCarthyism.

"Senators," White concluded, "I do not have answers to all these questions I have raised to suggest to you that our current standards on bias and partiality need to be analyzed and defined more precisely than they presently are. Currently, different Justices might have decided to recuse themselves, or not, for good-faith conclusions that other fair-minded people would disagree with. We all want objective Justices, judges with no personal ax to grind or direct economic or personal interest in an outcome. But which of us don't, deep down, really have developed ideas and positions on most of the issues that arise on the Supreme Court? Do we want Justices who come to decide momentous and consequential cases with *no* background or developed positions?" He added, modestly, "When a case arises in a field one of us has no expertise in—anti-trust or patent cases, for example—we end up following the lead of our colleagues who do."

He continued, "The Alliance for Justice, which represents over 130 civil rights and civil liberty organizations, has published a commentary that makes several wise recommendations. It suggests that written opinions about recusal challenges be decided not by the Justices themselves. Supreme Court recusal requests demand transparency and independent decisions. It pointed out that 4–4 split decisions, while rare, occurred 6 percent of the time since the recusal law was passed in 1974—32 times in 567 cases.

"Other federal judges follow ethical rules that are clearer than ours. Logic and common sense point in the same direction—no one, Supreme Court Justices especially, given that our power depends on the public's trust in our fairness—should be the sole judge to police their own official behavior.

"Our majestic building has on its facade, Equal Justice Under Law. Our integrity before the public requires that in fact and in appearance our work transcend partisanship and personal bias. Our decisions about contentious issues cannot bear scrutiny if the public does not respect and believe in our judiciousness and probity, and the morality of our decisions. Currently, our decisions about recusal challenges are not reviewable or sanctionable. That kind of aloof mysticism about judges is no longer acceptable."

Decorous, Justice White did not mention specific recent cases where Justices had taken questionable positions. But he did refer to the Alliance for Justice report and a Stanford University Law Review article, soon to be a book, which did cite specific instances and specific Justices.

Summing up, Justice White mentioned several alternatives consistent with the independence of the judiciary and setting reviewable independent oversight of recusal challenges. "It could be by a panel of circuit court judges—though that might be awkward to be judged by inferior court colleagues—or even better, by a retired Supreme Court Justice, or a neutral arbiter or some ombudsman figure with impeccable credentials—a position the same recent Stanford Law Review article recommended. The author is the Chief Justice's about-to-retire clerk, I should add."

At that, Justice White concluded, gathered his papers, smiled at the Chief Justice, and looked over his shoulder to Jake and Sydney, who returned large nods and smiles.

"Justice White and Chief Justice Freeman," the chairman stated. "You have raised so many fair and challenging questions that I suggest that the Court suggest to us how S.455 could be modified to accomplish the goals I believe our body and your

Court agree to. We respect your collegiality in bringing these problems to our attention. These issues Justice White raised can best be resolved with your Court's input and our oversight. We will reciprocate by working with you to assure the best recusal law going forward."

With that, he peremptorily stated, "The Committee is adjourned."

Sydney and Jake had come to the hearing, sitting in front-row seats reserved for guests of the panelists. After the testimony concluded, they stood and waited at the witness table, while the Chief Justice and Justice White gathered their papers. Then the Justices approached the senators as they stood to leave with their omnipresent staff assistants, to greet them, shake hands, and say friendly farewells. Attending reporters approached the Justices, hoping for printable remarks for the next day's papers.

To their surprise, Dennis McCarthy walked up to Jake as if they were old friends, and said, "Jake, your Justice made a lot of sense today." Jake didn't know how to respond without getting into more trouble with Justice White, as had happened the last time the two had encountered each other informally.

"Thanks," was all he could muster, looking over intensely at Sydney, seeming to say, *Don't go away, I may need a witness.*

McCarthy, noticing this tense moment, said, "What's the matter, Jake, I don't bite!"

"I've been bitten before. Not again," Jake answered curtly.

"Aw, come on, grow up. I wrote nothing that was wrong or not your own words. There was talk all over town about Justice White's relationship with the president when the announcement about that book first came out. Reporters report about public figures all the time, usually with the gratitude of the leakers, who want their turn to talk." He walked away, shaking his head.

Later, Jake, Sydney, and their Justices left Congress and returned to the Supreme Court dining room, the place where they all had met as strangers almost a year ago. Now they were lifelong colleagues, having earned their impressive new status.

The next day, McCarthy had a front-page piece about the Justices, quoting some of their testimony before Congress, quoting from Justice White's remarks, and praising the Court for surfacing an important issue and offering wise solutions to the troubling recusal law.

"Did you see the front page of the *Washington Post* today?" Sydney texted that morning. "I thought you didn't trust him?"

"How the town works, I guess," Jake replied.

chapter 23

Getting Even

Maybe Jake was learning how Washington worked, after all. He was rankled when Yancy outplayed him on the media politics of recusal, but too busy to do anything about it. But the idea about turning tables struck him when his old law school friend, Jeffrey Rosen, called to say that he and a colleague who worked with him at the ACLU headquarters in New York City were coming to Washington to interview a group of bureaucrats about a voting rights case their office was handling.

"I'd love to see the inside of the Court," Jeff mentioned. "Might we have lunch when I'm there and I could pick you up, see your digs?"

"Better than that, I'll reserve a table here and we can have lunch, on me. The menu is simple, but cheap," Jake added.

Two weeks later, when Jeff arrived, and after Jake—now the veteran insider—showed him the quick tour of his office and the surroundings, they sat in the same dining room where Jake only months ago had sat and auditioned with Justice White when he'd first visited.

When Jeff mentioned he was disappointed to have missed the Justice's speech at New York University when Jake had been in town, the idea popped into Jake's mind.

"That reminds me," he ad-libbed. "I've wanted to tell you a story your organization will be amused by." Jake told the story of the Conservative Society episode between him and Yancy.

Jeff, who was a good, rising political operative himself in his work, reacted as Jake expected.

"I'll be goddamned if the ACLU will partner with these guys, especially on our issues. We are against censorship; they were for it. We think the idea of self-pardoning is ridiculous, and they only believe conservative presidents should be able to pardon themselves."

"I thought you'd think that," Jake answered, smiling. "I have an idea how you could trump, to use a bad word, his play."

"How so?"

"Well, you're an NYU law alum. You may have missed the Justice's speech, but you read about it in the New York press the next day. Before the Conservative Society calls you about collaborating on the recusal reforms, why doesn't the ACLU co-opt them?"

"And how do we do this?"

"Give the Justice a public kudo, maybe an award for his act of judicial integrity. Do it before the Conservative Society can claim joint plaudits with the ACLU about recusal reform."

"We could do that."

"Better do it soon, before you find yourself in bed with the Conservative Society," Jake added.

"So now I know what the label 'Washington lawyer-insider' means," Jeff continued. "You are a smart fellar."

They left after Jake paid, they hugged, and the old pals went their separate ways. A few days later, standing with the NYU Law dean, the head of the ACLU main office in New York City held a press conference. "We honor our celebrated alum, US Supreme Court Associate Justice Richard White, on his leadership on the question of judicial ethics. Anyone who heard the Justice recently when he spoke at the NYU School of Law was edified by his non-partisan and judicious testimony. The

ACLU has written to the Chief Justice and Justice White him-self, praising his idea and awarding him a plaque today for 'his efforts to reform the Court's recusal laws.'" The press reported the announcement and gift givings.

On the Justice's behalf, Jake accepted the small plaque that was awarded to the judge for his work. The announcement did not mention the Conservative Society's original recusal threat in its letter. The recusal reform movement was suitably one for which Justice White and the ACLU could claim *all* the credit.

Jake called Dennis McCarthy at the *Post.*

"What's up, Jake?" Dennis asked.

"I may have a story for you," Jake whispered, conspiratorially.

"Listen to who's playing the Washington game now," Den-nis joked.

"Can we meet somewhere private?" Jake asked.

"Sure, where and when? It has to be before ten o'clock if you want it in tomorrow's paper."

"How about we meet for a drink at nine tonight, at my condo, the Pendleton."

"Ok, see you then, Deep Throat, not in your garage," Dennis kidded and hung up.

At nine sharp, Dennis arrived at Jake's place, and after enter-ing they sat at Jake's dining table, where he had assembled the announcement Jeff had prepared for the ACLU to release the next morning. Dennis asked when the release would come out. Jake told him noon.

"That works," Dennis replied. "I can submit it tonight for release online for publication at noon tomorrow. The New York papers will have to run it later in the day. Where will the press get it?"

"At the ACLU offices in New York City," Jake answered.

Dennis gathered the papers, smiled at Jake, and rose to leave. "Welcome to the NFL, buddy," Dennis remarked as he left Jake's apartment.

Jake got an email from Yancy the next day, reading, "We decided we have better cases for recusal. But always open to collaborating with you. Congratulations."

Yancy was a game player, who was played, not a sulker. There would be other times, other intrigues, he knew. Better to be a good sport than a sore loser.

chapter 24

Drake's, Again

This time, it was Jake who texted Sydney. "Can you meet me at Drake's tonight?"

"You splurging, Jake?" Sydney texted back. "What's the occasion?"

"You'll love it. Show up at seven."

When they arrived and were seated, they each ordered a drink. Jake had a sheepish look. Sydney was quizzical. "So, what's up?" she asked as they waited for their menus.

Adding drama, Jake did the same thing Sydney had done earlier. He slid a letter across the table and sipped his gin as Sydney put down her wine glass and read.

At one point, she looked up at Jake, jumped around the table, and noisily hugged him, to the delight of the people at nearby tables, shouting, "Jake, I'm so happy for you! For us! You've accepted? We can go together?" Sydney had never been so voluble, so excited.

"If we can go as husband and wife," Jake smiled.

"Yes, yes. Tell me all."

"Well, it turns out San Francisco doesn't have any law firms with a Supreme Court practice. Appellate, yes. Supreme Court, not yet. Big firms in big cities are doing that, to keep their clients from going to Washington for big-bucks, big-issue cases. San Francisco doesn't yet. Brock and Arguelo—a classy, boutique firm—want me to start it, keep up recruitments from the Court by going to Washington annually. I'll be doing other appellate trial work, but this new feature of their Supreme Court practice is why they are paying me the rate of third-year associates. I may make enough so we can get you preg—"

Sydney interrupted. "Say no more. Here's to us!" They clicked glasses and sat back silently, smiling. A woman observing the action from a neighboring table asked if they'd like her to take their picture with their iPhone. They did and posed again in an embrace, glasses raised. That punctuated their evening.

Their future was clear for Sydney and Jake now, at last, and their conversation about "what next" moved from abstract to very particular. Dinner lasted a long time as their conversation effortlessly moved to the real details of this new chapter in their lives, together and far away from the nation's capital. Neither of them would remember what they ate, but they sat at their table for hours engaged in making plans, in a sweet moment of their own.

No longer was their marriage an if, but rather when and where and what and who. This part came easily, was fun, and would continue in spare moments when the Court's active season drew to a close in late summer. They would marry early in September—before classes started—at a charming, boutique hotel in Palo Alto that Sydney loved. The guest list would have to be small because of their limited budget (her family would be guests, not hosts) and the fact that their invitations went out near the last minute. Ann would host a small celebration party for the Gang of Twenty.

Sydney handled the nuptial details. They used the picture their tablemate at Drake's had taken of them embracing after the proposal dinner on their invitation. (It would become their family heirloom.) Jake promised to get his family across the country on time, barely. There was no time to argue or worry about details, given the distances of the families, emotionally and geographically. They would tell their fellow clerks and their Justices right away, but would work on the details, guest list, and menus in the weeks that followed, as the Court's work continued after its annual summer break.

Sydney went to California when Court transitions and moving plans were complete. She was publicly ushered into all the faculty precincts. Jake went to New Jersey to pack and send to California what personal items he would keep. Then he went to Palo Alto after a stop in San Francisco to meet the people he'd be working with at his firm. He'd look for an apartment with Sydney, who would drive up from Palo Alto to join him. With their pooled resources, Sydney bought a small Chevy convertible that would be their first joint investment. Jake made the down payment for their lease (none before had been reviewed by this level of lawyering).

chapter 25

Happy Ending

The small wedding took place several days later at the sunny restaurant garden in Palo Alto Sydney had reserved. Jake's family and Sydney's had different attitudes about their children's marriage. Sydney's older sister, whom she rarely saw and Jake had never met, lived in Seattle, another world, with her husband and two children. Their schedule wasn't open for the surprise wedding. None of Sydney's family came except her parents, alone. The Emersons were miffed it was not to be an Episcopal wedding. Jake's parents were exultant, starting to think of names for their first grandchild. Only a few of his New Jersey family and old friends had time or funds to come across country at Jake's sudden invitation. Few of his old Jersey boys knew Sydney or were part of Jake's new life. "They probably think Sydney is a guy and this is a gay marriage," he joked to his parents. Formal announcements were sent to the Chief Justice and Justice White as a courtesy, with no expectation they would attend.

The night before the wedding, after a hectic day of last-minute arrangements, as they were undressing for their last night together as singles, Sydney and Jake had their first near-family quarrel. Sydney was upset by her parents' coldness toward Jake. Jake was his typical generous, glass-half-full self, replying, "Syd, don't let them spoil this for us. I'm not angry, so you needn't be." Sydney took his peaceful offering the wrong way, feeling responsible for her parents' misconduct when Jake's had been so sweet to her.

"Do you always have to be so freakin' cheery?"

"What, you want me to revile your mother and father, soon to be mine—kinda?"

They both laughed at this, and embraced.

"Jake, I love you. Let's get married."

"I'm free tomorrow!"

All the last-minute news wasn't irritating. To their great surprise and excitement, the Chief Justice had called to tell Sydney that he would officiate if she asked, and of course, she did. He would be en route to a judicial conference in Tokyo, and the date worked. He would travel from Washington to San Francisco, drive to Palo Alto, and officiate that evening, then depart for Japan the next morning. When Justice White heard about that, to Jake's delight, he deputized himself to join the ceremony.

It was to be a strange mix. Few family—one cold and on strike. Few contemporaries, though a few of their close Court colleagues did come from various cities across the country. Sydney's roommate, Ann, also teaching now nearby in San Diego, was the maid of honor. Ed Alderman, one of Jake's colleagues from his new law firm in San Francisco, came, but while they were paired to work together, they only had known each other briefly. Jake had not asked any of his Court friends—none were lifelong, as with the New Jersey ties that had faded over the last decade while Jake was away—to be best man. When Justice White heard that and learned that the Chief Justice would be there to officiate, he volunteered to fill the role. Jake was thrilled.

The wedding was small but classy, and with two Supreme Court Justices in attendance, the local press reported. They included a photo of the couple with the two Justices. What was a big deal in Palo Alto was just a gossip tidbit in the Washington press. The whole afternoon was sunny, cheery, elegant, and brief. Two musicians Sydney knew at Stanford played Vivaldi for a while when drinks were served, and Brubeck after, as people mingled, nibbled, and embraced the newly married couple.

When the outside ceremony ended on the flowery deck and champagne was served, the Chief made a toast. "I know both of these newlyweds and admire them hugely. The Mensa IQ of the West Coast goes up significantly now that, regretfully to us easterners, Jake and Sydney have moved here. Until they both return to the Court as Justices themselves." At this, there was some applause, and as many "no's" and "boos."

"Someday, no doubt, a PhD candidate will write a dissertation on Justice White's and my opinions and the impact of these two lovers on them. Don't believe a word of it," the smiling Chief added. And then he concluded, "On a more serious note, as a special gift to both of them, my colleague and I have a present for them."

In a ta-da, exaggerated gesture, White brought the Chief a package, which he slowly, clumsily unwrapped. It was a leather-bound volume of Sydney's new book, *On Judicial Ethics*. Attendees all applauded as Jake shook Justice White's hand while Sydney hugged the Chief.

The next morning, the weary but happy couple flew from San Francisco to Maui, where they spent their first week living together as man and wife. "I haven't brought any work with me this time," Jake teased, as they boarded their flight.

"Nor I my lecture notes," Sydney answered. "I found a used copy of Deborah Dawson's *Deserted* on Amazon!"

"Great," Jake smiled. "Maybe it will turn you on."

"You turn me on, big fella," Sydney replied.

"Perhaps you might even say this week we are recused?" Sydney grinned, and together they both laughed.

Epilogue

PublishersMarketplace

Recusal by Sydney Emerson

Book review by Alistair Robinson

In a new book from Stanford University Press, assistant law professor Sydney Emerson, a recent addition to Stanford's esteemed law faculty, writes about the troubling question of recusal, a subject at the center of Washington politics in recent years.

Recusal is what public officials do to take themselves out of power in situations when they have, or appear to have, conflicts of interests in making judgments. That classic but infrequent issue suddenly became newsworthy in the early Trump administration when the present attorney general, Jeff Sessions, recused himself from leading the investigation of foreign interference in the presidential election between Trump and Hillary Clinton. Sessions's recusal angered the president, who eventually fired Sessions and replaced him with a relatively unknown, unimpressive lawyer as interim attorney general, who himself had voiced opinions about the investigation indicating bias. That action caused wide public denunciations, media speculations, and public examination of what government recusal procedures are and ought to be.

That brouhaha was followed shortly after when the controversial appointment of Brett Kavanaugh to replace his mentor,

Epilogue

Californian Anthony Kennedy, became a cause célèbre. So many recusal motions were made against Kavanaugh by law professors who had criticized Kavanaugh's appointment and later had cases before the Court that the newly convened Democratic Congress began impeachment proceedings and Kavanaugh resigned rather than undergo further embarrassing hearings about his youthful "indiscretions." Kavanaugh joined an international law firm that represented, among other corporate giants, the largest brewery in the world. He was replaced on the Court by DC circuit court judge Merrick Garland.

Emerson's book exposes the hypocrisies of past recusal practices, focusing on the judicial system, and recommending reforms, some of which have already been undertaken.

A valuable read for the public, as well as for lawyers, legislators, and judges.

Publishers Journal gives *Recusal* three stars. ★ ★ ★

Alistair Robinson is a professor of law at the University of Virginia, who reviews regularly on judicial affairs.

Acknowledgments

My thanks and gratitude to my able and versatile colleague, Gerrie Sturman, and to my ever helpful and energetic law clerk, Maddie Greathouse, and to Stephanie Beard, my enthusiastic editor.

About the Author

Ronald Goldfarb, Washington DC attorney, author and literary agent uses the pseudonym R.L. Sommer to distinguish his fiction (*Courtship* was his first novel, published in 2015) from his extensive (13 books, 600 articles, reviews, and op-eds) non-fiction work.

While *Recusal's* analysis of the legal issue at the heart of the novel is accurate, the story is made up, as is the dual theme, the love story between two central characters. The idea for the book derived from the notorious Senate confirmation hearings of now Associate Supreme Court Justice Brett Kavanaugh. While some of the Court characters in Sommer's novel are real, their roles are fictional here, as is the love story, completely.

Sommer will write a sequel Turner will publish, *The Gender Wars*, involving the two central characters in *Recusal*, as that story might evolve twenty years after *Recusal* which is written in the present. *Recusal's* relevance will be clear as the subject of the title is arising increasingly in media.

Goldfarb has practiced law and been an active literary agent in Washington, DC for decades and writes with an insider's view of how dramatic stories evolve in the nation's capital. He has served the courts and Congress as special counsel, private organizations (Brookings) and federal and state government agencies, has hosted a Public Broadcasting System program, *Devil's Advocate* (WETA), and presided over the work of MainStreet, a television production company, on award winning programs. He has argued in the U.S. Supreme Court, and had personal and professional dealings with some of its Justices.

Sommer (Goldfarb) studied at Syracuse University (A.B., LL. B.) and Yale Law School (LLM, JSD), worked for three years as a trial counsel in the U.S. Air Force JAG Corps, and for Attorney General Robert F. Kennedy for four years in the Justice Department prosecuting organized crime cases and in New York as Kennedy's speech writer in the 1964 election.

His website (www.ronaldgoldfarb.com) lists his many writings and unique role in public affairs to the present. "In 2019, at its sesquicentennial anniversary Syracuse University awarded him and his architect wife its highest, distinguished alumni award.

Turner will also publish Goldfarb's forthcoming book about the Ethics of Lawyers later in 2020.